LOOSE ENDS

Prospectus

Loose Ends

BRIAN D'EON

RESOURCE *Publications* · Eugene, Oregon

LOOSE ENDS

Resource Publications
An Imprint of Wipf and Stock Publishers
199 W. 8th Ave., Suite 3
Eugene, OR 97401

www.wipfandstock.com

PAPERBACK ISBN: 978-1-7252-7143-2
HARDCOVER ISBN: 978-1-7252-7142-5
EBOOK ISBN: 978-1-7252-7144-9

Manufactured in the U.S.A.   JULY 1, 2020

Loose Ends is a work of fiction. The dialogue between characters is mostly an invention of the author. Where Scripture is quoted directly, it is indicated by italics and double quotation marks, or rendered as blocked quotations. All biblical quotations are taken from:

The New Revised Standard Version Bible: Catholic Edition, copyright 1989, 1993, Division of Christian Education of the National Council of the Churches of Christ in the United States of America. Used by permission. All rights reserved.
For the purposes of narrative flow, the author paraphrases when necessary.

For Judy

And we are put on earth a little space,
That we may learn to bear the beams of love.

—*William Blake*

Contents

Introduction and Invocation

Thank you, God, for creating a knowable universe. Thank you for the gift of a transparent atmosphere that reveals stars. Thank you for the laws of physics which allow us to glimpse the eternal blueprint. Thank you, God, for creating minds that allow us to generalize, to find patterns, to make predictions and, most wonderfully, to imagine.

Holy Scripture is a multi-layered source of wisdom and inspiration that invites exploration. For me the Bible is full of patterns and meaning yet to be discovered. As a writer, it is a place where I may apply my imagination in hopes of finding new avenues to express my gratitude, and deepen my connection with the Creator.

Judaism has a long history of connecting imagination and Scripture through the tradition known as midrash. Midrash stories can be fantastical, profound, pious or even satirical. Midrash writers try to make Old Testament stories more meaningful for a people far removed from the time in which these stories were originally written. Often story details are expanded, as authors try to fill in the gaps or tie up "Loose Ends."

Christianity has its own (much less well known) midrash literature tradition. Its stories have much the same purpose—in this case, to make *Jesus* more meaningful to a modern audience. Midrash literally means "to seek" or to "conduct research." Writers of such stories have treated the books of the Bible as fluid sources, ripe for investigation, contemplation, expansion and re-interpretation. In these stories, piety and imagination find a place to live creatively together.

Contents

With joy (and some trepidation) I have put these stories to paper, confident that Holy Scripture is easily robust enough to withstand the imaginative assaults of writers like myself who, like blind men surrounding an elephant, attempt a description of the indescribable.

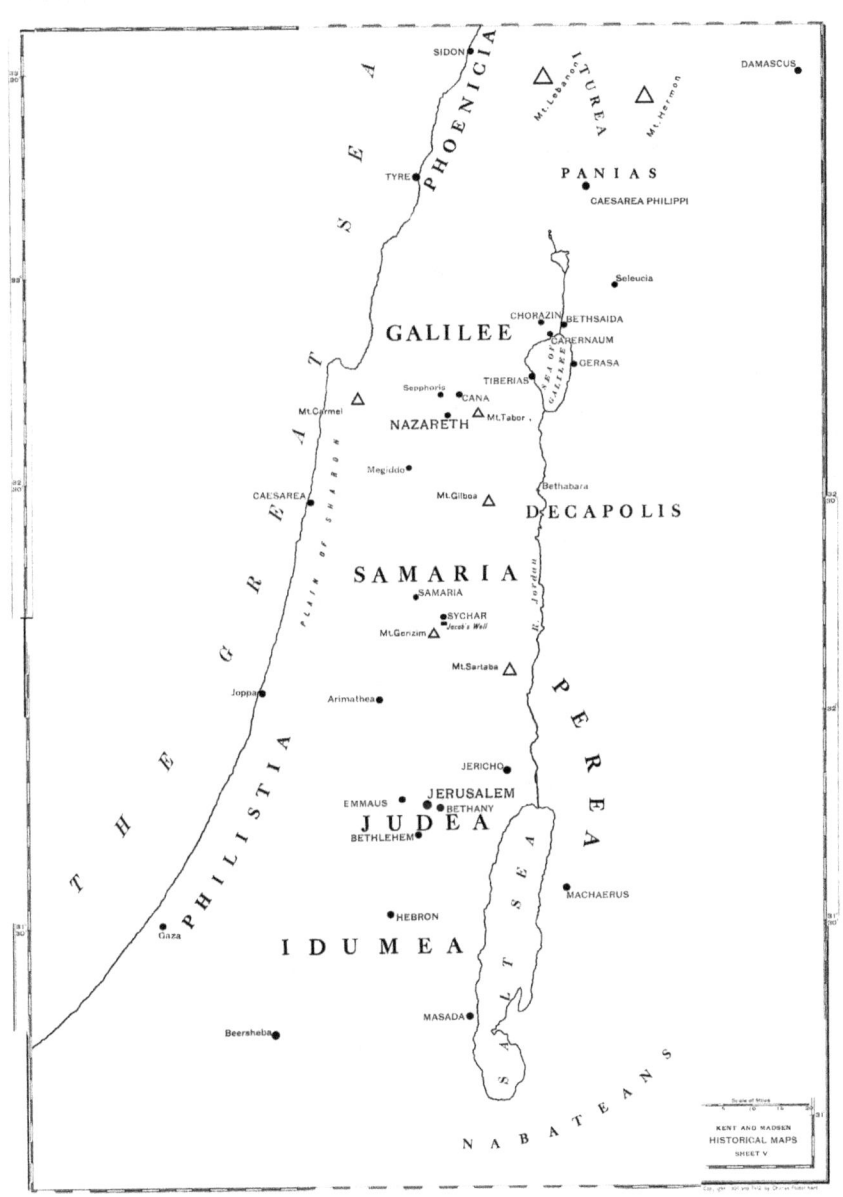

SIDON

DAMASCUS

Mt.Lebanon

I. T U R E A

Mt.Hermon

P H O E N I C I A

TYRE

P A N I A S

CAESAREA PHILIPPI

Seleucia

CHORAZIN BETHSAIDA

G A L I L E E

CAPERNAUM

GERASA

Sepphoris

TIBERIAS

CANA

Mt.Carmel

Mt.Tabor

N A Z A R E T H

Megiddo

CAESAREA

Mt.Gilboa

Bethabara

D E C A P O L I S

S A M A R I A

SAMARIA

SYCHAR

Mt.Gerizim

Jacob's Well

Mt.Sartaba

P E R E A

Joppa

Arimathea

JERICHO

S A L T   S E A

EMMAUS

J E R U S A L E M

BETHANY

BETHLEHEM

J U D E A

MACHAERUS

HEBRON

I D U M E A

Gaza

MASADA

Beersheba

N A B A T E A N S

T H E   G R E A T   S E A

P L A I N   O F   S H A R O N

P H I L I S T I A

R. Jordan

S E A   O F   G A L I L E E

Scale of Miles

KENT AND MADSEN

HISTORICAL MAPS

SHEET V

PALESTINE IN THE TIME OF JESUS, 4 B.C.-30 A.D.

(INCLUDING THE PERIOD OF HEROD, 40-4 B.C.)

Road Trip

Through the tent's opening, Melchior peered at the distant tan-colored dunes that subtly changed shape even as he gazed. He had loved this landscape from his youth, ever seduced by its simplicity and the way it focused his thoughts. "Well?" he asked, turning back to his colleagues, "any mistakes?"

What was there for Melchior to be anxious about? Had he not counseled kings and advised generals? All thanks to the heavenly stars and his gift for interpretation. But, as for the task before him *now*, his powers of prognostication seemed quite inadequate.

For more than an hour, Balthazar and Gaspar had been examining the astrological chart. It was some of Melchior's finest work: a white vellum parchment, exquisite in detail, festooned with beautiful symbols and figures, all artfully arranged over a large table.

Mostly the two magi nodded; often they rubbed their chins or helped themselves from a bowl of figs. Buxom serving girls were never far away, ready to refresh their drinks, yet never—not once—did the two scholars look away from their work. "I can find no mistakes," Gaspar conceded.

Head hovering a few inches above the document, Balthazar stared intently at the Sumerian symbol for the planet Venus. His eyesight was beginning to fail. For a magus such as him, this was a great misfortune—yet he never complained. "Two years before the conjunction, you say?"

Melchior approached his friend. "With a margin of error of one month, either way."

The half-blind Balthazar lifted his head and smiled. "A remarkable alignment! The planets will appear as a single star if your calculations are correct."

"They *are* correct."

"The gods willing, we shall see!" A small hint of irony crept into Balthazar's voice, as if he knew very well that, in two years time, he might not see at all or, if he did, with such poor resolution that, to him, *any* close points of light would appear as a single star.

Gaspar asked, "Could we not study the conjunction just as well from here?"

Melchior knew only too well that his interpretation was based on the synthesis of clues from many unrelated documents, one of which spoke of a king in the land of Judah and his association with the Celestial Fish. Taken individually, no textual clue was definitive, but taken cumulatively, they formed a line of reasoning as straight and irresistible as a bronze-tipped arrow—or so Melchior was prepared to argue. "Yes, Gaspar, we *could* study it from here, if it were not for my dream."

"Your dream?" Balthazar said, "Why did you not tell us?"

Melchior interpreted the dreams of others fearlessly—more often than not, successfully—but when it came to his *own* dreams—often poorly remembered—he regarded them as inconclusive, sometimes misleading.

He struggled to look his colleagues in the eye. "I could see the three of us riding camels in a land that was not our own."

"Which land?" Balthazar asked.

Melchior's head waggled in a gesture halfway between a nod and a shake. "I could see palm trees, goats, and distant sheep. In many ways, it resembled home, but then we passed by a great sea such as I had never seen."

Balthazar's foggy eyes lit up; perhaps he was thinking of his home on the shores of the Caspian. Melchior felt a need to elaborate: "Or perhaps it was merely a very large lake."

Gaspar steered them back on topic: "What else did you see?"

"One man I could see very clearly—a soldier. I can even remember the words he spoke; he turned to another beside him and said, '*Ubi sumus nunc princeps?*'"*

Gaspar raised his eyebrows. "Latin?"

"I believe so."

"So," Balthazar mused, "we're headed for Rome?"

"Or *somewhere* in the Empire, at any rate," Gaspar said, "which doesn't exactly narrow it down."

---

* "Where are we now captain?"

"I only know that my dream tells me we must head west, and it's from there we shall see the great conjunction—which, of course, is only a sign of something much greater."

Gaspar scrunched together his lips and put his hands behind his back. It was his turn to stare outside the tent's entrance and into the sandy distance. "And does your dream tell us when we must begin this journey?"

"We should have begun already."

There had been great wailing and gnashing of teeth as Gaspar, with six wives clinging to his limbs, trudged his way toward the camels. He did not look back; he barked orders to his servants, and in two great shakes, freed his limbs and mounted the lead camel. "Forward!" he cried. The shout echoed down the line, doing its best to rise above the ululations of grieving women. "Forward!"

"We'll be back before you know it!" Melchior had said to his own wife, his *one* wife—he was eccentric that way. But Melchior knew the words were hollow; he did not believe them himself.

Balthazar was last, saying goodbye to sons and daughters and a great gaggle of grandchildren, laughing as he did, as if ready for one final adventure and wanting to relish to its utmost, beginning, middle and end.

Turning, Melchior shouted out behind him, "It's not too late to change your mind, Gaspar!"

Stone-faced, his colleague answered, "Four years free from my wives? Make it eight and I am a happy man." He thumped his feet against his camel's sides. "Lead on, my friend!"

They found safety in the company of other caravans heading west. Nevertheless, their numbers dwindled steadily as different groups veered off toward their own particular destinations. Danger followed them everywhere: from wild beasts, famine, disease, and the ever present threat of thieves and murderers. They were encamped not far from the Tigris River one night, when Gaspar's man single-handedly killed four bandits who had slipped into their camp.

The three magi stared at the corpses. "That might easily have been us," Gaspar remarked.

"It *will* be us, one way or another," Balthazar replied. "A man's days are numbered. One cannot escape one's fate."

Melchior smiled weakly. "And yet today we seem to have done just that. Thanks to . . . ?"

"Simbu," Gaspar's man replied, wiping his wet knife blade on the grass. Was this man an *enemy* of destiny, Melchior asked himself, or one of its agents? He turned to his faithful friends. "I'm so sorry for having dragged you into this."

Gaspar and Balthazar waved off the apology, acting as if night attacks by thieves were trifles and the journey they had undertaken a mere afternoon amble.

The next year of travelling brought many more close calls. They encountered sand storms twice, even snow on one occasion, and once had to fend off a lion. Scattered everywhere along their route were government officials eager to be bribed. This, thankfully, they had anticipated. But now their store of gold coins and fine spices was nearly spent.

Finally, after one year and eleven months, they arrived at Melchior's great sea—the Sea of Galilee, the locals called it, although it was not salty. All the same, they were very encouraged to see it and know that Melchior's dream had substance.

For several nights, the magi sat by their campfire and watched intently as the three planets did their dance, moving inexorably closer together. "I can see Venus," Balthazar declared, "but not the other two planets."

"They're there," Gaspar assured him.

Smiling, Melchior added, "It shouldn't be long now." Then he threw a twig into the fire and laughed.

"What's so amusing?" Gaspar asked.

"I can't believe we made it this far."

Gaspar laughed with him. "Nor I, my friend!"

"Clearly it has been the will of the gods," Balthazar said.

Melchior shook his head and stared into the fire. "I don't think my charts were quite as conclusive as I pretended."

Gaspar smiled. "It wasn't the charts."

"What then?"

"Your dream."

Embarrassed, Melchior looked away.

"Not just your actual dream, but your vision, the dream *within* you."

Balthazar elaborated: "We *trust* you, Melchior."

Gaspar nodded. "If you say we must go west, we go west."

Balthazar added, "If you say we must leave now, we leave now."

Melchior's heart beat faster, and a trickle of perspiration slipped from his forehead and stalled on his cheek. "But why should you believe *me*, ahead of your own good judgment?"

During the almost two years of trekking, Balthazar's eyes had grown steadily more glassy. It was a wonder he could see anything at all. "Because it is through you, Melchior, that the gods speak."

Ah! thought Melchior. They might have chosen a worthier vessel.

"But tell us one thing," Gaspar said. "You talked about a great event to coincide with the moment of the conjunction—perhaps it is now time to tell us exactly what we should expect."

Melchior squirmed, the soles of his sandals gouging small troughs in the sand. How could others be more confident of his dreams than he himself?

With excitement, Balthazar asked, "Is it a great king?"

Melchior squirmed even more. "In part."

"A great teacher? A prophet?" Gapsar ventured.

"That too, quite possibly."

"Well, what then?"

Melchior had no choice but to spit it out: "In my dream I saw a child."

Balthazar gasped, then laughed, but it was not a laugh of derision. "We have crossed the wilderness for two years in pursuit of a *child*?"

"But a child with *such* eyes, Balthazar! If only I could paint you a picture."

Gaspar rose decisively to his feet. Balthazar rose too, holding on to Gaspar's arm. "Extraordinary!"

In alarm, Melchior looked at his friends. "You're leaving?"

Speaking softly, Gaspar put a hand on Melchior's shoulder. "Which way, my friend? Clearly there is no time to waste."

Was Melchior imagining this? Was this another of his dreams? "South," he answered, stammering slightly, "Toward Jerusalem." Gaspar couldn't possibly be suggesting they travel *by night*? "But we can wait for dawn, surely."

Suddenly a group of six armed and mounted men appeared. Three of them held lit torches. They spoke in Latin first, then switched to Greek. Not bothering to dismount, the leader said, "Welcome to Galilee. Surely you are the three magi we have heard so much about."

"You know who we are?"

"The King of Judea has many ears. He has heard of your renown and begs an audience so he may share in your wisdom." With a large hand wrapped in a thick leather glove, the leader pointed southwards. "If you would be so kind."

This was more than a simple request, and the three magi looked at each other, wondering how best to respond. The clink of bronze swords against scabbards brought them to a quick decision.

"Come," the captain called out, the same *princeps* Melchior had seen in his dream, "King Herod awaits!"

Mute

Sighing, Elizabeth looked at her husband. How had Zechariah grown so old? In the last few months his hair had turned from merely gray to now snow white. This, and the loss of his power of speech, had been much remarked upon. He'd had a vision. Visited by an angel, one of the village priests had explained.

Whatever had happened that day, Zechariah had gone into the temple one man, and come out another. "Like Moses," her neighbor Hannah had said to her. Elizabeth nodded but said nothing; her husband was no Moses.

Rising slowly from her chair, Elizabeth put one hand on her belly, the other on her back. "Don't worry, husband. I won't be long." The baby inside her was up to its old tricks: slapping like a fish and swimming back and forth. It made Elizabeth laugh to see her swollen fingers bounce into the air.

"Do you understand me?" Elizabeth had asked when she first learned of her husband's affliction. He nodded vigorously. "Are you well? Apart from your voice?" Tears began to stream down Zechariah's sunken cheeks. Elizabeth led him home. For the next three days he did little except sleep. When he woke, he would try to speak, but could manage only an indistinct rasp, usually followed by coughing and more tears.

It was embarrassing to think how long it took for Elizabeth to give her husband a tablet to write on. At first he had used it frequently, writing feverishly. He wrote the word "angel" repeatedly and the word "son," and underlined both words, connecting them with a thick line. He did this so consistently and insistently that Elizabeth began to wonder if what the old priest had told her could be true. That miracles still happened. And her husband had been witness to one.

A few short weeks later, Elizabeth experienced a miracle firsthand— one she could barely bring herself to believe—she was pregnant, despite being far past child-bearing age.

Her husband mute, herself pregnant—there must be a connection, though what it was she dared not imagine.

For five months Elizabeth stayed indoors, just to be certain. She had no trouble guessing what the village women were saying: *First Zechariah struck down mute, and now Elizabeth stricken with who knows what terrible disease—what great sin had brought down such judgment upon them?*

Mostly Elizabeth cooked, sat in her chair, cleaned, sang, and rested her hands upon her belly. One month, two months, three months—she had no particular sense of time passing beyond the rising and setting of the sun, the cycle of Sabbaths, and the very gradual growing of her belly. Then, one morning, very suddenly, she knew the time had come. Smiling, she rose from her bed. She opened the window shutters fully, splashed water on her face, combed her thick, long hair (one blessing old age had not taken from her), then tied it neatly behind her neck. She was twenty years old again. Twenty, but with aching knees, stooped back, and wavering voice. None-theless, a glorious second heartbeat fluttered inside her like a tiny bird.

Taking advantage of her husband's weakened powers of protest, Elizabeth quickly covered her head and stepped outside for the first time in months. Sparrows greeted her and the aroma of wild sage and olive oil. Her neighbor Hannah's two young sons were in the middle of some game that involved running in a circle around the nearest adult. Once done, they squealed in delight and ran off looking for their next victim. "Blessings, Moshe! Blessings Aaron!" But as Elizabeth cried out, the children were long gone, leaving behind a laughing trail of dust.

Elizabeth made her way to the village center—carefully, deliberately, step by step, moving closer to that chatter of voices she had so desperately missed. She could hear them all. Clucking like chickens, beloved chickens: her friends, her neighbors, even women with whom she normally wouldn't talk. And she could hear the voices gasping, and see the fingers pointing, and finally—after explaining her long absence—a dozen smiling faces sur-rounded her. "Elizabeth!" they screamed. "What miracle is this? The Lord is great indeed!" And soon she was the center of a mass of hands and fingers which stroked her hair and patted her belly, and lips that kissed her on the cheek. And, of course, the women made her sit almost at once. They brought her water and fruit, and the air was filled with impossible questions that fell upon her like a cloud of ravenous starlings.

"Are you well?" they asked.

Yes, yes, she was well, though not for the first few months. But now she was very well—had never felt better.

"When is the joyous day?"

"In four months." Even as she answered, this did not seem possible. Maybe the baby would be born tomorrow, maybe in ten months—who knew what the Lord had in store for her? Elizabeth could imagine herself being pregnant indefinitely, and it was not an unpleasant thought.

"When your time is near," her neighbors explained, "you will be more than happy to have it over and done with!"

"Boy or girl?" another asked.

God's joy would reside in either.

"Would you like us to tell you?" A great huddle of old women began to argue over which was the most reliable method to foretell the child's sex, but Elizabeth stopped them. "Really, I don't wish to know. The Lord's will be done." She laughed, and it was as if sunbeams shot from her lips. "Though, for Zechariah's sake, one might dare hope for a boy."

From this day on, Elizabeth made daily walks to the village center, her waddling gait and smiling face settling into a synchronous rhythm with the arcing sun.

The walk had become her favorite part of the day. Elizabeth was just about to step out again when she heard an urgent knocking at the door. It was twice-blessed Hannah. "Elizabeth," she cried, "you have a visitor!" Hannah pointed toward the village center where Elizabeth could just make out a small cloud of dust and hear a commotion of voices. "Your cousin from Nazareth!"

"Mary?"

"She'll be here any minute." Hannah squeezed Elizabeth's arm and retreated. "Aaron!" she called out, "I told you to leave those chickens alone! And stop teasing your brother!" The clucking of bird and mother merged into one, and soon, deep in thought, Elizabeth heard nothing at all.

Why had Mary come? She was a sweet girl, but it had been years since Elizabeth had seen her. And what was this fluttering in her belly? Not the usual—much more insistent. And why did her feet seem stuck to the floor, not allowing her to move? She turned to her husband. "Our cousin from Nazareth—she's here."

Groaning, Zechariah rose from his chair.

"You've always liked Mary, haven't you?"

Zechariah smiled widely, as if the mere mention of his cousin's name somehow untangled a puzzle or promised some sweet resolution.

Through the open door, Elizabeth could see Mary making her way past the well and the throng of curious women. Goodness! thought Elizabeth. Her cousin was now a fully grown woman. So much taller than Elizabeth remembered. And pretty, but in a quiet way. What Elizabeth most remembered about her cousin was her eyes—beautiful eyes—green—and almost frightening in the way they could look right through a person.

Elizabeth laughed, recalling their last meeting—how serious young Mary had been. Courteous to a fault and kind, but *so* serious. How wonderful to learn that she had married Joseph, the carpenter, a good man by all accounts—Mary would have settled for nothing less.

What a smile her cousin had! It was like the sun rising; Elizabeth could think of no other way to describe it, and then she remembered how Hannah had described her own face in just such a way. "Elizabeth!" she had said, "I can tell you are with child, just by your smile!"

Before Elizabeth was quite ready, Mary stood there at the door. The floor seemed to drop away, and the baby inside Elizabeth jumped and kicked and banged with two fists. "Oh!" cried Elizabeth, dizzy suddenly, and grabbing the side of the door for balance. Was this what it was like for her husband in the temple? Maybe she too was about to be struck dumb! What would the two of them do then?

But that was not the plan. . . . All at once the flood gates opened and words poured out like a mighty river. "Cousin!" Elizabeth cried out, "how glad I am to see you! *Blessed are you among women!*"[1]

For a brief moment the two cousins lived in God's timeless universe: past, future and present all melted into one. More than talking to each other, they sang.

From a quiet corner, trembling slightly, Zechariah looked on. Smiling like an infant, he took a first halting step, then another—growing more confident with each one.

Words! Where were the words he wanted to say? Tears streamed down his cheeks as he went to greet his cousin. He groaned, he mumbled, he made no sense at all and yet it was as if one of the bright ones had touched his shoulder, encouraging him. Welcome Mary! Welcome, dear cousin! Welcome, mother of our Savior!

Zechariah's steps quickened, his smile brightened and, for the first time in many months, his tongue fell loose and words began to spill.

Ambition

"No, no, that's fine." It was rare for Joseph to interrupt, but he had heard enough. "I understand." Random words dribbled from his mouth. "These things happen."

But could such a thing happen to *Mary*? Only now did Joseph have the courage to look fully into his betrothed's eyes. What was he to make of what he saw there? It wasn't shame—what was it? He saw tears, clearly, but not for herself; were they for *him*?

Quickly Joseph refilled his bucket, concentrating on the hand-over-hand action of hauling the vessel upwards from the well. "I have to get back to work." With the bucket at its apex, and water weeping from its sides, he paused and turned to Mary. He had to duck his head to catch her eyes. He rested his bucket on the ground and forced a smile. "It is a simple thing. We call off the betrothal, no harm done."

The sun blazed high in the sky and seemed reluctant to move, overheating Joseph's thoughts as he worked in his shop. He filed, he sawed, he hammered. The day would not end, and it was almost the greatest surprise of his life to find himself at last in bed, oil lamp by his side, sighing, staring up at the ceiling. He guessed he would never fall asleep. Yet Yahweh had other ideas.

Next thing Joseph knew, his eyes snapped open. He was awake and eager. At most, a dozen times in his life had he experienced a sleep so refreshing, so restorative, so—he could not find the word. He knew only that this day, like no other, promised to be wonderful which—considering what had just passed—was surprising.

Joseph sat up. He laughed to smell the straw in his bedding, the cool earthy smell of adobe, the sweet smoke of a morning oven. From outside he heard the bray of donkeys, the cry of roosters, the twitter of song birds flitting among the branches—all making him want to rush outside and join in the joyous cacophony. Yes! Joseph thought—he could imagine himself standing on the street, crowing with the roosters. *That* would be a sight to remember—but what would Mary think of him?—howling like a madman.

Except . . . it probably didn't matter anymore.

It made no sense—it was almost aggravating—how could he feel like this—so full of energy and confidence?

Joseph threw off his blanket and stood, wiggling his fingers and toes, surprised and delighted to find no stiffness in them. Perhaps he was not old after all. He'd heard the whispers, of course. "He's too old for Mary," they said. Others argued in his defense: "Yes, but he'll be a good provider." This was true. "And since when did age have anything to do with it?"

It was a fair argument. Joseph's own father was just as old when he married—there was nothing in the least unusual about it. "But Mary's only a *child*," he'd heard others say. In age perhaps, but there was something about Mary. She was mature beyond her years, and when she smiled, it was not the smile of a child—it was ageless. It was as if, within her heart, she held secrets no one else in Nazareth had the least inkling about. Sometimes it unnerved Joseph. Always it drew him to her. Like a moth to a flame, his friends had told him.

Again, none of this mattered—not now.

Joseph stepped outside. The sun was a hand's width above the eastern hills. His neighbor, Amos, was already loading his cart, getting ready for the market. Of course Amos knew nothing about Joseph and Mary. Why should he? "Good morning, Joseph," he called out, not too loudly, letting those still asleep enjoy their blessed time. "It will be hot today."

Joseph inhaled deeply, savoring the scent of mountain thyme. "I think it might."

Amos placed the last of his produce in his cart, then tapped his sleepy-eyed donkey on the backside, urging it forward. Joseph listened to the sound of the ancient wheels press over the dust and pebbles, a sweet climax to the symphony of the waking town. "Remember, Joseph, don't work too hard." Amos waved, didn't look back. The day had begun in earnest.

"Don't work too hard." The words rang in Joseph's ears and made him squirm and search for something to do with his hands. For really, these words meant just the opposite, didn't they? It was a joke. Hard work and long hours are what defined a craftsman. But did they, really?

Should one judge a man's worth by how many hours he labored? How much he produced? How much he sweated? Till this moment, Joseph had never really given any thought to this question. Always his guiding principle had been only to make the work *good*. Time, price, satisfaction, all these were secondary to the compulsion to make the work *good*. For by the product of his hands, did not a man give glory to God?

And yet, it was such questions that stung his heart most. "Joseph is a good man," they would say, "but he has no *ambition*." Again, Joseph asked himself, what did this mean? Was Joseph to make more tables than the next man, ask for higher prices? Was he to be something more than the carpenter he was? Was he to be a rabbi too? Should a donkey aim to be a horse? What *was* ambition? Maybe, thought Joseph, it was nothing more than dissatisfaction.

Where did this leave Joseph? He was happy in his life. He loved his village. He loved his work. He loved his family and neighbors. And he loved the young woman he was promised to, except—Joseph sighed and shook his head—soon he would be betrothed to no one; he could put it off no longer.

What Joseph hated most was the whispering—the suggestion that somehow he might have done better than take *Mary* as his wife. After all, who was Mary? Her family was nothing special—not from the house of David, like Joseph himself. Despite being only a carpenter, *that* distinction they could never take from him. But no—they misunderstood completely—he respected their views, grey beards and all, but they were as wrong as they could be. There was so much more to Mary. Why could only he see it?

A gust of wind made the door to his shop creak, and Joseph turned around to see a shaft of sunlight shoot into the darkened room. Dust motes danced in the air along its path, and Joseph gasped at this sudden apparition of beauty. Then it struck him—as abruptly as a wooden beam across his forehead—he *remembered*.

How was it possible he could have forgotten! *Last night.* He'd had a dream—and such a dream! The Torah spoke of such things, but to think it should happen to Joseph of Nazareth, a mere carpenter, a nobody without ambition!

"*Joseph*," the angel had said. The creature was all light, all warmth, and spoke in words that seemed to wrap round him like a mother's embrace. "*Joseph, son of David, do not be afraid to take Mary as your wife.*"

Joseph remembered laughing out loud and shaking his head. The angel wagged a finger at him and continued: *"For the child conceived in her is from the Holy Spirit."*[2]

So *that's* what was in Mary's eyes!

"She will bear a son, and you are to name him Jesus."

Yes, yes, of course. Jesus, it will be!

"For he will save his people from their sins."[3]

Joseph could feel his heart pounding. It felt as if a nest of chattering sparrows were in his chest, clamoring to be set free. He strode toward the door, skipped past the shaft of light and into the full raucous color of the early morning.

By now, the town had fully woken, everyone busy, some walking downhill, others up. "Have you seen Mary?" Joseph asked, hardly stopping to wait for an answer, following a line of laughter and fingers which all pointed to the town center. And praise his Heavenly Father, there she stood! Waiting her turn in line, holding a jug in one arm, a basket in the other.

Joseph grinned broadly as Mary placed her jug on the ground. His heart beat faster and faster, and it seemed like minutes since he had last taken a breath. "Mary!" he yelled out, waving, dodging between the crowd of mostly women. "Joseph!" Mary called back, uncovering her head and mirroring his grin.

In a moment, Joseph stood by her side. The sun shone behind his head like a heavenly aureole, like the fires of divine ambition itself. He grasped Mary's hand, not caring that he did so in full public view. "Mary! I know what we must do!"

Look Up

"I tell you, my friend, sometimes the stars do indeed fall from Heaven. I have seen it."

Their small fire crackled and the scent of cypress wafted into the night air, tugging at Enoch's heart. The scent reminded him of home, of his boyhood, of the days of scampering beneath the palms and chasing the family chickens, the goats, the young lambs—whatever dared cross his path. Back then, the animals had been his playthings; now they were simply—well, much of the time—burdens.

Life in general—most of the time—a burden.

Aaron resumed his argument: "You need only look for yourself, Enoch. I see them almost every night."

"See what?"

"Stars! Falling from Heaven! Have you been listening at all?"

Enoch picked up a stone and examined it, as if appraising its usefulness. He tossed it downhill. He could hear it bounce against other rocks as it went on its zigzag journey through the darkness, its final resting place forever unknown. "If the stars were falling from Heaven, Aaron, would there not be fewer and fewer every night? Would the sky not, by now, be empty?"

Enoch risked a glance up, daring the Creator to contradict him. But nothing had changed. As always, the pattern of the stars was as unwavering as holy writ.

"Enoch, who is to say that our Lord does not make *new* stars to replace the ones that have fallen?"

The sheep grazed downhill from them, assembled in two loose groups, barely discernible as lumpy silhouettes against the light of the distant town.

"I've never seen Bethlehem like this. Why are there so many lanterns, do you think?"

Enoch cared little for speculation. He answered Aaron grudgingly, "Visitors?"

"Visitors from where?"

"Didn't some Romans come into town the other day?"

"What do the Romans want with Bethlehem?"

"I'm a *shepherd* Aaron. Like you. How would I know what the Romans are up to?"

Little neck bells sounded as one group of sheep drifted left, close to a small cliff. Enoch jumped to his feet and whistled loudly, but the sheep paid no attention. Enoch grabbed a stone and hurled it between the sheep and the cliff. "Stay!" he yelled.

"Stupid sheep," he said—but in a whisper, too superstitious to risk offending the source of his livelihood. Enoch shook a fist and delivered another piercing whistle, till finally the sheep obeyed, backing up and finding a safer place to graze.

Moments later, they heard footsteps.

"Enoch! Aaron!" The voice gradually grew louder as its owner climbed between the two groups of sheep.

"Samuel!" Aaron answered. "Where have you been? It's the second watch already."

Standing in front of the fire and panting, Samuel explained, "My wife. Sorry."

"Ah!" Aaron exclaimed. "We understand."

Aaron and Enoch spoke in teasing unison: "*Newlyweds.*"

Samuel sat heavily on the ground and wiped his brow. "It can be exhausting!"

Enoch clapped him on the shoulder.

"*Fixing our home!*" Samuel explained. "Moving furniture, cleaning, rearranging." Samuel struggled not to smile: "What did you think I meant?"

All three men laughed and looked into the fire. The aroma of cypress momentarily strengthened as a fresh branch collapsed in the flames.

"Samuel?" Aaron asked. "Is it true about the Romans?"

Samuel pulled a piece of cheese from his pocket, passed it around, and began to chew. "They're everywhere. Can't take two steps without bumping into a Roman. A *census*, I think they call it. They have tables set up in the main square."

"So now they are *merchants* as well as soldiers?"

Samuel shrugged. "For some reason they want to count all of us."

"So they can tax us better, yes?"

Already the Romans taxed them to the limit. What more could they want? Did they expect blood from a stone?

"But I tell you, my friends," Samuel resumed, "these days it is much better to be up here than down there. What with the Romans, the merchants, the innkeepers—you can hardly move or hear yourself think. Anyway," Samuel squinted, looking through the darkness," I have always much preferred the company of sheep."

"Amen," Aaron said. Enoch kept his opinion to himself.

"Look!" Aaron called out suddenly, pointing upwards.

"What?" Samuel asked.

Enoch would not look; instead he rolled his eyes and shook his head. "Another of Aaron's 'falling stars'. Or so he insists on telling me."

"You always miss them!"

"Maybe, Aaron, because they are not there."

"Or maybe, Enoch, because you never look."

Aaron sighed, but to Enoch it did not seem an expression of frustration. It was how you might react after seeing a beautiful woman. A sigh of sweet desire or—more than that—adoration.

"Do it for me," Aaron pleaded. "All I ask is that the two of you seriously look. For once."

Enoch had never seen Aaron quite so earnest.

"Just lay your heads back on the grass and *look*."

"The grass is damp and cold."

"Oh, for the love of the Holy Temple, Enoch, put a *blanket* under your head!"

"And get it all dirty?"

"Arrg!"

After a suitable pause, allowing the frustration to subside, Enoch asked, "Where should we look?"

"Anywhere! Just up. Let the Heavens do the rest."

No one spoke. The firelight illuminated their grey breath which drifted lazily up toward the stars. All too soon, Enoch declared, "I see nothing."

"Hush!" Aaron answered, "Keep looking."

More time passed. Several hundred heartbeats, at least. Enoch began to squirm and scratch himself. "I need to check the sheep."

"Just a little longer," Aaron insisted. "Usually they are much more frequent."

Enoch rose to his feet. "Enough, Aaron."

But then, all words, thoughts, and presumption fell away. The sky filled with light much brighter than the combined lanterns of all Bethlehem. It was light of a different quality, neither white, nor amber, nor any color at all—transparent and glowing at the same time.

Enoch gasped. "This is your falling star?"

Aaron could barely speak. "I don't know *what* it is."

Samuel grabbed his friend's arm. "*This* is amazing, Aaron! Why did you not tell us?"

Enoch tried to regain his feet, but couldn't. He could do no better than the others, sprawled on the ground, head craned upwards, bearing his weight on trembling arms.

"*Do not be afraid,*" the voice said. If it *was* a voice, it was *inside* them—as well as outside.

Like a bolt of lightning, a thought entered Enoch's head, a thought of such clarity that he laughed out loud. Yes! This was a message he had been waiting for his whole life: *Do not be afraid.*

Again the voice, the *voices,* the very sky, spoke: "*For see—I am bringing you good news of great joy for all people.*"[4]

Enoch's heart raced like the pattering hooves of a thousand sheep.

"*To you is born this day in the City of David a Savior, who is the Messiah, the Lord.*"[5]

"In Bethlehem?"

And the voice and light had form.

"A shining one!" Aaron cried out, and he was more right than he had ever been. The angel pointed downhill.

"*This will be a sign for you: you will find a child wrapped in bands of cloth and lying in a manger.*"[6]

Then the light of heaven doubled in depth and brightness, knocking the three shepherds flat on their backs.

Angels seemed to fill the sky—a host, a starry assembly, singing out their message:

> "*Glory to God in the highest heaven!*
> *and on earth peace among those whom he favors!*"[7]

And then they were gone, leaving behind only a single, bright star which, like a tear drop, fell in the general direction of Bethlehem. Finally, the three men rose to their feet, surprised they could do so. They brushed off their cloaks and wiped their brows. Speechless, Enoch put a hand on Aaron's shoulder.

"I know," Aaron laughed, grabbing Enoch's hand, "I *know*!"

Samuel was laughing too. "What do you know?"

"Very little! Except that we must go find this Savior."

Samuel looked left and right and up and down. "Right now?" he asked.

"Samuel," Enoch answered—a great flow of words ready to burst, thirty years of cynicism underfoot like condensing dew—"the sheep will understand!"

The three men strode downhill, each of them hoisting a woolly companion atop his shoulders as he went. "Hush now, my little friend," Enoch said to his bleating charge, "we are going to where the grazing is much better!"

"But Enoch!" Samuel protested, still unsure of this venture. Then Aaron tapped him on the shoulder and made him look behind. There, in a remarkably ordered group, the rest of the sheep were following.

Oil and Drool

"Am I in Sheol?" the dying man asked.

"Not yet," answered the spirit that floated above his bed.

"It *smells* like Sheol."

What the dying man smelled was his own putrefying body, and the gangrene moving up his legs, now *between* his legs, the agony and itching boring into his soul—if he *had* a soul—which was uncertain. It would be better if he hadn't.

"You are in your own bed," the spirit explained, "in Jericho."

"In Jericho? That piss hole?" The dying man struggled to sit up, but the pain was too much; he fell back, panting. "Masada, that's where I am, right? The fumes, the heaviness of the air. I am no fool; I know the Salt Sea when I smell it!"

Without answering, the spirit slowly began to drift.

The dying man cried out, "Did I say you could leave!"

A physician stood beside the dying man and wiped his brow, then moved to soak up the drool pooling on his chin. The dying man pushed the hand aside. "Spirit, I command you to stay!"

The spirit would not be commanded. Nevertheless, she hovered and paused.

"And don't think I don't know that voice!" The dying man thrust an accusatory finger into the air. "I have heard it many times! I *know* you!"

Still, the spirit would not answer.

Known to the outside world as Herod the Great, the dying man violently grabbed hold of his physician's arm. "Do you think this is a child's puppet show? No one is to be by my bedside except my inner circle. Did I not make myself clear?"

Occasionally Herod's pronouncements were lucid, but often they were not, and it was a challenge beyond the skills of a stuttering Greek physician to know which were which.

"Great Lord Herod," the physician asked, "whom do you wish us to remove from the room?"

"Look at her!" Herod declared, pointing up. "Butter would not melt in her mouth—nor will she speak when commanded!" One of Herod's eyes was swollen almost shut. It made his face even more threatening than usual. "Was it *you* who let her in?"

"No, great Lord!" the physician answered. "There is only the inner circle, as you directed." Helplessly the physician followed Herod's finger to the ceiling.

"Send her away at once!"

The physician's name was Socrates, and at this moment, he might have welcomed a cup of hemlock if it were offered. Desperately he looked for intervention from someone in the inner circle. None was forthcoming. Herod's two sons shrugged and smirked. The king's sister simply shook her head.

"Shoo! Shoo!" Socrates said, moving his hands in a vaguely circular motion, hoping this was an appropriate gesture for exorcising apparitions.

"No, wait!" Herod cried out. "The spirit shall not leave before explaining her presence!" Again Herod attempted to sit up. He screamed in agony, but would not be denied. Regal orders demanded a regal posture. "Spirit, I say! What do want with me? Tell me who you are!"

The spirit moved closer, hovering just out of reach.

"Why do you torment me?"

There could be no mistaking the face. It was a beautiful face, an extraordinary face, a face that, even after all these years, haunted Herod's dreams—his one true love, Mariamne, whom circumstances beyond his control had forced him to execute.

"Mariamne!" the king cried, turning his head, looking away. Spittle and blood fell onto his pillow. Socrates moved to wipe the king's lips, but again was pushed away. "How was I to know, Mariamne? How? Everywhere a king is surrounded by enemies. How was I to know?"

The expressions on the faces of the two brothers changed from snickers to sneers. It had all happened long before their time, but they knew the story well. How their half-brother, Antipater, had spread rumors about the loyalty of the king's golden boys, Alexander and Aristobulus. And good old

Antipater, first-born (but not first in succession), not content with simply ruining the hopes of Mariamne's sons, did in Mariamne herself. He accused her of adultery.

There could be only one end to this story. Herod the Great executed all three of them—the boys first, then their mother.

"Mariamne!" Herod cried out again, sobbing and spitting up more blood. "Forgive me, Mariamne! It was Antipater who made me do it! Damn the boy! Lies! Lies! Nothing but lies! Why will no one tell me the truth?"

The two brothers—not sons of Mariamne, of course, neither the first nor the second—looked on in restrained amusement. The old man was dying. Of this there could be no doubt. But the will was not in force quite yet. Neither Archelaus nor Antipas wanted, at the last moment, to upset their prospects.

Archelaus whispered to his younger brother: "Antipas, do you know what they say about him in Rome?"

Antipas snorted. "I imagine they say many things."

"They say 'better to be Herod's pig than his son!' "

The saying was as true as it was comic, but until the old man rested safely in his tomb, they must maintain at least the appearance of mournful offspring.

In the mind of Antipas, it was this obsession with *offspring* that was at the heart of all the family's troubles. The old man simply could not give his royal member a rest. Married ten times! Sired eight sons (that Antipas knew of) plus a half dozen daughters. Did he expect the sons would somehow learn to "get along"?

It drove Antipas to distraction—how people would go on and on about what a clever administrator his father was, how he had the Romans in the palm of his hand, how he had consolidated his kingdom, how Herod's great building projects had endeared him to the people.

Endeared? Really? The man was a monster. And getting worse with age. If only they would give the reins to Antipas—*he* would show them how to run a kingdom.

Archelaus turned to look at his brother who, as usual, seemed lost in a daydream. Poor, old, deluded Antipas—the *good* brother, as he was fond of calling himself. He had no idea, *no idea*! Herod had made a *new* will only the day before. Safely hidden behind a curtain, Archelaus had overheard the whole business. He struggled not to laugh as he heard his father dictate new terms to a trembling Greek scribe.

The new will stipulated that his little brother (who had long regarded himself as the rightful heir) would now receive but a small portion of the kingdom—Galilee, a backwater. Meanwhile, Judea and Idumea would go to Archelaus.

"Mariamne!" the great king cried out, reaching up into the air, longing for an embrace. And then the spirit did something very unexpected; it divided itself in two. Herod was confused at first, but soon the meaning became clear. Above him floated *both* Mariamnes, wives Two and Three. A new flood of tears washed down the king's pock-marked face. "Mariamne! Oh my Mariamnes! If only you had said something! If only Antipater. . . ." The king couldn't finish. His grief was too great, and his agony rose to a level he formerly could not have imagined.

Recalling his family's sordid history, Antipas could only shake his head. The palace intrigues in Rome had nothing on his father's. It wasn't enough he should kill his beautiful Mariamne, but then he took to wife a *second* Mariamne, also a beauty.

King Herod clearly had some regrets about how he'd handled things with the first Mariamne. He seemed determined to behave better. He fathered another son and called him Herod II, making his intentions for the boy transparent.

Antipas's prospects might have ended then and there (before he was even conceived), had it not been for first-born Antipater once again sowing doubts—his particular genius. In several subtle ways, Antipater sullied the reputation of young Herod, the so-called Second. Best of all though—and here Antipas could not restrain the full smile that lit up his face—his good old half-brother, Antipater, finally ran out of patience, and tried to poison the king! Poison! *A woman's weapon!* Did he really imagine the king, with all his spies, would not uncover the plot?

Apparently, Mariamne II knew about the plot as well—though she did not share this knowledge with her husband.

Antipas smiled grimly and shook his head. The woman should have counted herself lucky to escape with her life. And her son too, for that matter. Herod II was not involved in the attempted assassination (he was living in Rome at the time); nevertheless his mother's disgrace doomed any hopes he had for future advancement. Mother and son were exiled to Gaul—a backwater if ever there was one.

So, who was left? Antipas, of course—the *good* brother. He understood well enough he would have to give his older brother *something*, some position of importance or *apparent* importance, but what Israel needed, above all, was a steady head and hand; Antipas had both.

Confident and ruthless, the two brothers turned to look at each other, smiling for entirely different reasons.

"Doctor!" Herod cried out. "The pain! It's worse!" The king reached up to grab the physician's tunic, using all his strength to hold on. "They told me you were the best! They were wrong! You have done nothing for me!"

Gently, Socrates lifted the royal fingers from his tunic. "Lord Herod, there is one other thing we could try."

"Anything!"

"A hot oil bath to help restore the balance in your humors."

"Do it!"

"It is already prepared, your Excellency."

Quickly two Idumaean slaves helped the king from his bed. A six-legged monster, they staggered toward a tub. Rising hot vapors added a new layer of mist to Herod's already milky vision. The two Mariamnes continued to float above him, tantalizingly just out of reach.

"Mariamne!" Herod cried out, but more faintly now, his cries interspersed with coughs and spits.

They stripped the king of his robes. He was more spoiled meat than man. With the greatest of efforts, he lifted one discolored leg, then the other. The slaves guided him into the greasy liquid. Herod screamed in pain. His legs were on fire. So too were his eyes as he looked up at the two Mariamnes who were smiling at him, two tranquil phantoms. Then they turned and kissed one other on the lips.

"Ah!" Herod screamed, the pain unbearable.

Hand in hand, the two Mariamnes gently began to recede. Following them were Herod's two beautiful boys, Alexander and Aristobulus, their heads remarkably re-attached. "My sweet, sweet boys!" Herod cried, his voice thin and cracking. "I was wrong about you! How was I to know?"

All Herod's limbs were screaming and his scalp seemed ready to ignite. A messenger came rushing to his side. "Your Excellency! I bring news!"

Herod's teeth were chattering, as if he were encased in ice. "What news?"

"It has been accomplished, my Lord, just as you commanded. All Bethlehem's male infants have been killed."

Herod could vaguely remember some such thing. The details eluded him.

"And we did this because . . . ?"

"Because of the prophecy that a new King of the Jews would be born there."

Herod nodded his head. It took a concerted effort and all the focus he could manage. "Well," he said, looking not at the messenger, but straight up, wondering if he would ever again see his two Mariamnes. "That's that, then."

"I regret, your Excellency, we had no success in tracking down the magi."

Herod squeezed his eyes shut—partly in pain, partly in frustration. Not every plan could be brought to fruition.

"And the two hundred? What about the two hundred?"

Only Herod's sister seemed to make sense of this reference. She came to her brother's side: "All in our custody, Lord Herod, only waiting the sad moment of your passing."

"And then they shall be killed."

"As you instructed, dear brother."

Herod managed one final nod; he was not sure he could manage another. "And then there shall be mourning throughout the land." (Not rejoicing, as he feared.)

Herod looked back at his two sons. From this distance he could not tell who was whom. "You'll be happy to see the last of me, won't you, boys?" There was no answer. Herod let his head slip beneath the oil.

In a Strange Land

The size of the river still amazed Joseph. Locals told him its source lay far to the south in a mountainous land at the edge of the world—at a distance much further than any man could walk. Or would *care* to walk, Joseph might have added, vividly recalling the blisters on his feet after his family's hasty flight from Bethlehem.

Half daydreaming, Joseph gazed out at the seemingly endless parade of river boats, their bright sails glimmering in the water's reflected light, suggesting the flittering wings of butterflies. The boats were heading north—their final destination the Great Sea whose extent was almost beyond imagining.

Joseph shook his head; he was too busy for such daydreams. Just surviving was a fulltime job: looking after his young wife and toddler son—it was no easy thing. It was hard to find work, especially for a carpenter in a land without wood. And yet . . . somehow there *was* wood. Many of those boats Joseph gazed upon carried strange timbers in their holds. Dark, dense cuts such as Joseph had never seen. In what kind of a land did such trees grow?

"Come, Jesus," Mary called out, her voice light and lilting, like the breeze that blew in off the Nile. Jesus ran toward his mother, returning her laugh. He ran everywhere, as if this were a requirement of toddlers—never walk when you could run. And if the boy had been blessed with wings, he would surely have taken flight, and *then* what would they do? Joseph joined in the laughter. His son's merriment was infectious, and the smile it brought to Mary's lips touched him deeply.

Life in Egypt was hard, but it had worked wonders for Mary. It was as if she had cast off a great weight from her shoulders. Here she could truly be young again. Here her marvelous son could run free—and Mary seemed untroubled by the day-to-day hardships of life as a refugee. "God will provide," she'd said to Joseph, putting her hand on his—smiling, reassuring him, when surely it was *his* job to reassure her.

"Don't worry!" Mary had said, just the other day, her face beaming for no obvious reason—except, of course, for the presence her son who was reason enough for everything. "We won't be here forever, Joseph!"

This statement only made Joseph imagine they *might* be there forever. If any place made a man consider the idea of "forever," Egypt was it. One just needed to look at the pyramids. Even from here, a good thousand cubits away, they loomed above the horizon like great knuckles punching up from the underworld. Who knew how old they were? Or how long they would last? And who could believe that mere mortals had constructed them?

Joseph thought of his namesake, that famous ancestor who, like him, had been abandoned in the desert—thrown to the bottom of a well, left there to die—and yet, even when all had seemed hopeless, Yahweh had intervened.

But he was not *that* Joseph, and Pharaoh could have little use for a lowly Jewish carpenter.

"You are Parthians, yes?"

To Joseph's ears, the words were gibberish till the young boy repeated them, this time in Greek, of which, over the years, Joseph had acquired a passing knowledge.

The voice belonged to a young Egyptian, ten or eleven years old, Joseph guessed. Standing atop a small sand dune, he looked down on them, his perfect white garments gleaming in the morning sun. "Wait," the boy said, bringing a hand to his forehead to block the sun's glare. "On second thought, you must be Jews, correct?"

Joseph fell to one knee and bowed. "Yes, your Grace." Mary waved her son closer. Jesus giggled and dashed back to his mother.

The mini-Pharaoh took large, confident strides down the dune. The grains of sand parted obediently before him. "My father says there are many Jews in our land. *And* Parthians, *and* Medes *and* Cretans. People from all over the world. Why is that, do you think?"

"I do not know, your Grace."

"It must be because, of all the lands in the world, Egypt is the greatest—there can be no other explanation."

A tuft of grass, tenaciously rooted in the parched soil, quivered in the breeze. The boy stood behind it, as if in charge of its movement.

"Ah! You have a boy!" the Egyptian exclaimed.

"Your Grace, allow me to introduce our son, Jesus."

Jesus squealed in delight, wriggling in his mother's arms. Mary held him tightly.

"You Jews have funny names, don't you?"

Joseph nodded, said nothing.

"But my father says Jews are hard workers." The boy looked over his shoulder. "There is a story that some of your people even helped construct Khufu's tomb—but it is just a story." The boy smiled, then waved back a braided lock of hair which blew across his face. "We have so many stories—they cannot all be true."

Abruptly the boy clapped his hands. Almost at once, a servant appeared—until now hidden from view behind the dune. The man was very tall, and as black as the dark northbound timbers coming up the Nile. More incredible still was the animal he held by a leash.

It was a large cat, strangely marked; its legs seemed surprisingly spindly. Egypt was full of such oddities.

"What do you think of my cheetah?" the boy asked.

"Cheetah," Joseph echoed, doing his best to get his tongue around the exotic syllables.

The boy laughed. "Do Jews have cheetahs?" He looked over at Mary and Jesus. "I expect not. How could you?"

Again the young Egyptian clapped his hands, in a manner subtly different than before, for the servant seemed to understand immediately what he was to do. He handed over the leash to the boy who, smiling, began to parade his exotic pet.

Joseph gave the two a wide berth.

"Your boy would like to see my cheetah, yes?"

Jesus was all eyes.

"Do not worry, Jewess, the beast will harm no one while he is in my care."

Mary shot a glance over at Joseph, and in that brief moment, must have loosened her grip, enough for the giggling Jesus to step away from her. Mary brought a hand to her mouth, stifling a shriek.

"It's all right, Mary," Joseph said, assuming a confidence he did not truly have.

"Boy," the Egyptian called, "come closer."

Jesus did.

It was like the game of mirrors: Jesus stood erect, smiling at the cat. Each looked into the others' eyes. Suddenly Jesus plopped to the ground on all fours, head upright and back arched. The cheetah did likewise.

"He likes you!" the Egyptian declared.

Jesus laughed and jumped wildly. The cheetah jumped too.

The Egyptian lowered his head to Jesus's level. "What other tricks do you know?"

"Running!" Jesus replied.

Joseph translated, as Jesus raced around an imaginary circle, putting an end to any confusion the Egyptian might have about the boy's favourite "trick."

"Yes!" the Egyptian said. "It is one of my favorite things also!" He untied the cheetah's leash, and it dashed toward the river, passing over and around dunes, then into marshland and papyrus reeds.

Both boys laughed, the pitch of their voices not that different, when suddenly (without warning, as toddlers very often do), Jesus made a run for it. He moved as fast as his little legs would carry him, straight toward the river in pursuit of the cheetah. The Egyptian followed.

The cheetah was almost too fast for eyes to follow, a spotted, tawny-colored burst of fur, bounding in and out of reeds and grasses, causing shore birds to explode into the air at its approach.

Joseph and Mary could only watch. The minutes seemed like hours, especially when the boys were out of sight. But then they would reappear, always running, till finally Jesus answered his mother's prayers and steered them back to their starting point.

"*Imma! Abba!*" he cried out, beaming and muddy as he sat at their feet. "The cheetah is very fast!" Mary wiped her son's brow. Joseph passed him a cup of water.

The Egyptian too sat down, clapping his hands again. The servant stepped forward with a decorated ceramic jar. From it, he poured water into a bronze cup that was embossed with scenes of water birds and crocodiles.

The Egyptian smiled when he finished drinking. "Your boy is fast for his age!"

Yet more words for Mary to ponder in her heart.

The Egyptian looked back over his shoulder and whistled. The cheetah moved with falcon-like speed, and Joseph, despite his best efforts, could not help flinching when the animal came to a sudden halt, almost within arm's length of himself and Mary. Still, for the boy's sake, he must show no fear.

The sleek animal was panting rapidly and black tear drops seemed permanently etched beneath its eyes. Yet, to Joseph, the cheetah did not seem sad—quite the contrary. Joseph was studying the markings of this amazing creature so intently that he was shocked when suddenly he noticed a hand stroking its head—Jesus's hand.

Smiling, the Egyptian said, "Of very few people, does my cheetah allow this." Then the Egyptian too stoked the great cat's head. The cheetah blinked several times, then lay down, content to allow the stroking to continue.

The Egyptian rose to his feet as if struck by a great notion. "Of course!" he declared, stretching his arms to the wind. "I know what we must do next!"

Joseph could do nothing but take Mary's hand and hope for the best.

"It is a day for flying kites, is it not?" The Egyptian clapped hands again. The servant disappeared behind the dune for a good two minutes, then re-appeared with a heavily laden camel in tow. From one of the camel's bags, the servant pulled out what must be a kite. As a young boy, Joseph too had once flown a kite—fashioned by his uncle—but it was nothing like this. The Egyptian's kite was brightly colored in reds and blues and had gold-colored tassels hanging from its tail. On its back was the picture of a great bird.

The Egyptian leapt to his feet and seemed almost to sing to his servant: "Make Horus fly!"

Expertly the servant tossed the triangular kite high into the air, where immediately it caught the breeze. He handed the kite's hemp cord to his master.

"Look little Jew!" the Egyptian cried out. "See how high it goes!"

Jesus was on his feet too, jumping up and down and squealing in delight.

"Watch it soar, brother! Maybe we shall make it fly all the way back to Judea!" The Egyptian looked at the parents: "That is where you are from, yes?"

(Not exactly, but close.) Joseph nodded.

"And some day you will return there, yes?"

"We cannot, your Grace."

"Why not?"

"We would not be welcomed by the king."

No indeed. Herod, slaughterer of babies. No place for their son.

By now the hemp cord had stretched out to its full length. The kite was a mere dot in the pale, blue desert sky. "The King of Judea? Herod, you mean?"

Joseph nodded.

The Egyptian laughed long and as deeply as a boy his age could manage, as if he knew some day this would be required of him. "Kings come and go; did you not know this? Unless they are *Egyptian* kings." Joseph started as the Egyptian handed the kite's cord to Jesus. "Hold it tight, little brother. It likes to jump like a fish."

Hand on chin, the Egyptian turned back to the parents. "Herod, you say? Just a minute. . . ." He looked up to the cloudless sky, thinking. "I'm quite sure I heard my father recently speak of him—saying that he was . . . sick or something—no! Not that! He said that Herod of Judea had *died*! No more King Herod!"

The Egyptian patted Joseph on the shoulder, which was both alarming and welcome. "Now you may go home!"

There was a sudden gust of wind and a gasp from Jesus. The kite had proved to be a bigger fish than the boy could handle, and the wind had yanked the cord right out of his hand. Horus had broken free.

"Ha, little Jew!" the Egyptian said. "Do not worry yourself! There will be other battles to fight. And you are sure to win many!" He patted Jesus on the shoulder; then one more time, he clapped his hands. He and his servant headed back to the camel.

"Farewell, my Jewish friends," the Egyptian called out. "May the gods of Egypt protect you on your journey." Then he bowed low in a manner unexpected of a high-ranking Egyptian.

For Joseph, the incidents of this day were like an extraordinary dream. *All* his days in Egypt had this quality to them. Had they really been there at all? he would later ask himself. Had an angel actually spoken to him? And what did Yahweh expect of him next?

Then he would remember his father's advice from many years before. "Joseph," he would say, "about some things it is not profitable to speculate."

Next day, at first light, the family set out for Judea.

His Father's House

They were halfway back to Nazareth when they realized Jesus was missing.

"He's probably visiting one of his cousins," Joseph said. Shrugging and smiling, looking back at the great line of pilgrims of which they were but one small part, he put a hand on Mary's shoulder and did his best to be reassuring. "You know what twelve-year-old boys are like. Restless, always wandering here and there." Joseph even managed a little laugh. "Always looking for trouble."

But was this really an accurate description of Jesus? Their son, the trouble-maker? Hardly. Well, at least, not in the usual way. And, as for the behavior of twelve-year-old boys in general, Joseph could hardly base his judgment on his own experience. *He* had never been a trouble-maker. He had always done his best to stay close to home and family.

And so they searched and *searched*. "Have you seen Jesus?" they asked seventy times and more—seventy times seven. They received many pained smiles, many sympathetic shakes of the head. The women would hug each other, whisper prayers and reassurances, but no helpful information was passed on.

Mary finally declared, "Jerusalem! We have to go back." Then and there, she began walking—a trot more than a walk—even though it was late afternoon. Joseph scrambled to fill a bag with food and grab a water gourd—he had to run to catch up. It was uphill all the way to the sacred city, and it was hot and sticky. It took a monumental effort from Joseph to make Mary stop and rest.

"The boy knows how to look after himself," Joseph assured her as they sat beneath a palm, eating some figs and dates. Mary took only one bite of each. "Once we find him, I'm sure there'll be a perfectly sensible explanation for all this."

All this. What *was* all this? It was so long ago now that it seemed more like a dream than a reality—that night the angel had spoken to him, reassuring him that he should wed Mary after all, reassuring him that the child she was carrying was especially anointed by God and destined to save his people.

Joseph had always known Jesus was different. "Does *your* son do that?" he would ask friends and family, and sometimes they answered with happy nods, but more often with confused looks and a slow shaking of the head. After a while, Joseph stopped asking.

It was not like you could ask an angel questions—at any rate, at the time, Joseph could think of none. Afterwards though, he'd had many. How exactly would their son be a savior to his people, for example? And why did this news make his wife both ecstatic and deeply troubled?

Mary had had her own angel, though what he'd said to her, Mary mostly kept to herself. The shepherds of Bethlehem also had seen angels—a whole host of them—but couldn't agree about their message, beyond the fact that the angels had brought good news. And that, as one of the shepherds was eager to emphasize, "they should not be afraid."

It made Joseph's head spin to try to make sense of *all this.* Nonetheless, Joseph always had within him a deep sense of purpose and a certainty that his wife and son were destined for something extraordinary. Just to be a part of it, in even the smallest way, would be the greatest of honors. Still, there were so many unanswered questions.

Yet who was Joseph? Was he Abraham? Was he Moses? Who was he to expect the Book of the Holy One to be opened just for him?

After only a brief rest, Mary insisted they continue walking, even though night had fallen. Joseph would not allow it. Very few times in their married life had he taken such a stand, but it was too dangerous to travel by night; he could not, in all conscience. . . . But then, fortuitously (or just as likely by the act of an angel) a new group of pilgrims came by. They were friends of Mary's cousin, Elizabeth, and they too were determined to walk through the night. Mary's life seemed filled with such occurrences—"signs," she called them. This was yet another. For the first time in three days, she allowed a smile to creep across her face.

Morning had just broken when they entered Jerusalem. Joseph looked at the maze of streets, perplexed about where to start. "This way!" he said, deciding to try the first street they saw on their left. Together they marched, looking left and right, into every nook and corner, periodically calling out their son's name. Soon Joseph had broken out in a great sweat, far in excess of what mere physical exertion could explain. After only a few minutes, he stopped and declared with more false certainty: "No, I think the other way is better!"

Now Mary took charge. She put a hand on Joseph's arm to tell him as much. She looked to her right and had to choose among three streets that forked away from the square in which they found themselves. A bright spike of light reflecting off the gilt roof of the Temple made the decision for her. She pointed, and off they sped.

Joseph continued to query strangers, often walking backwards as he spoke, trying not to let Mary get too far ahead: "Have you seen our son? Twelve-years-old? About this high?" But all Joseph received were shrugs and curious looks.

They walked on. As they turned this corner and that, again the rim of the Temple roof would reflect the sun, beckoning them. "Have you seen our boy?" Joseph continued to ask, till finally, an older rabbi nodded and bowed, reason for Mary to come to a stop at last.

"You are the parents?" the rabbi asked. Grinning widely, the rabbi bowed again, and offered a blessing. "Yes, yes!" he said. "For the last two days he has been at the Temple praying with us, listening, asking questions."

"That sounds like our son!"

"But," the rabbi continued, "most astounding of all, are the answers he gave to the questions we put to *him*." The rabbi shook his head in clear wonderment. "How can a boy so young know so much?" The rabbi peered more closely at Joseph. "You are clearly a scholar, sir."

Joseph lowered his head. "Just a carpenter; I work with my hands."

The rabbi pulled the beard away from his lips, as if in need to speak with greater clarity, "Then holy must be the houses you build!"

By now Mary had exhausted her patience; she pulled at Joseph's arm.

"Yes! Yes!" the rabbi told them, laughing. "Go! Go! And blessings be with you!"

It was as the rabbi had described. A dozen bearded scholars sat in a semi-circle, their eyes and ears fixed upon Jesus who, seeing his parents, stopped in mid-sentence. "Mother?" he said. His voice was even and calm, as if he had just been in an adjacent room, and his mother had come to announce dinner was ready.

Mary frowned and wrung her hands. "*Child, why have you treated us like this? Look, your father and I have been searching for you in great anxiety.*"[8]

The scholars surrounding Jesus spoke in whispers and mumbles and pointed in the direction of the parents. "These are the parents!" one of them said. "And there is the father!" said another.

It took a long time for Jesus to answer his mother. Meanwhile, Joseph simply stared, trying to understand what was happening. There they stood in the Holy Temple, the most sacred place in all Israel. And there sat their son, commanding an audience of biblical scholars, as if this were an everyday occurrence for him.

Briefly, Jesus looked at Joseph, then back to his mother. He smiled quizzically, as if mildly surprised. "*Did you not know that I must be in my Father's house?*"[9]

Next in Line

A voice crying in the wilderness—that's what his friends had told him, and it was true. Here Ezra stood on a gently sloping hill, while below him, down by the river's edge, a voice boomed that could be mistaken for no other:

> *Prepare the way of the Lord;*
> *make his paths straight.*[10]

Again and again, as Ezra moved closer to the front of the line, he heard these words. He felt slightly uncomfortable that the line was so sinuous, not straight at all.

"Repent for the kingdom of heaven has come near."[11]

Could the Baptist's promises be true? Ezra asked himself. That a man could start his life anew! There was so much in Ezra's life he regretted, wished he could undo. Could the waters of the Jordan somehow free him of his sinful past?

Ezra looked down at his weathered hands. Sometimes they seemed not his at all; it was as if they had a mind of their own. His hands had blood on them, had participated in actions which were shameful, unmentionable, more times than he wished to remember. Why did he always repeat the same mistakes?

"I baptize you with water for repentance."[12]

Most of John the Baptist's words were loud, brash, meant for all to hear, but *these* words, delivered at the very end, were spoken tenderly, as if delivered by the tongue of a young woman. Someone like his mother, or his sister—both gone.

It confused Ezra—this melding of ferocity and gentleness. But the worst—for Ezra anyway—would be the immersion. As a boy, he had almost drowned in a river; as a man, he had done his part to make sure another man did. The man was a thief and a Gentile. Still, to hold a man's head under water, to watch the last bubbles of air escape from his lips, to feel his flailing arms and legs suddenly go limp and his eyes grow vacant. . . . If Ezra never stepped into a river again, it would be too soon.

"*Repent for the kingdom of heaven has come near!*"[13]

On the Jordan's opposite bank stood the already-baptised. The "saved," he'd heard some people call them. Ezra had his doubts, but there they stood: chirping like birds, hugging each other, their heads and clothes still wet. Maybe people *could* change.

Ezra's heart beat faster when he saw that only two men remained between him and the Baptist. The very sky seemed to echo his concern. Like ships of war, the clouds sped by, threatening rain. Their shadows raced across the hilltops, plunging the land into darkness, then into light. A strong wind followed, making palm fronds flap horizontally and men hold up their sleeves against the swirling sand.

The Baptist did not waver. "*I baptize you with water for repentance.*"[14] His voice grew hoarse, and Ezra feared it might not hold out long enough for *him*. Like his thoughts, the weather was capricious; the wind began to flag and the clouds to part, allowing a single shaft of light to fall on the Baptist and the man he was about to immerse.

Ezra was growing impatient; it should have been his turn by now, but the Baptist seemed in no hurry, seemed to be slowing down intentionally. He just stood there, frozen, exchanging whispers with some stranger. Finally, he disrupted the ritual completely by dropping to his knees so that only his shoulders and head stood above the water. What was he doing? It was almost if the Baptist *himself* were preparing for immersion.

A crack of thunder caused a flock of small birds to explode from a nearby tree, and the rain began to pour. Great drops bounced at odd angles off the pilgrims' heads. The line scattered, men heading for shelter under the nearest trees, but Ezra held fast, protecting his place in line.

The Baptist did not move, nor did the man who stood before him. The roaring rain fell in great torrents, causing the river to rise visibly. A single cone of light persisted, continuing to shine on the two river-sodden men.

With bent head, the Baptist said, "*I need to be baptised by you, and do you come to me?*"[15] Then he rose and cautiously placed his hands on the stranger's shoulders. Ezra mouthed the words with him: "*I baptize you with water for repentance*"[16] A thunderous clap and rumble followed, drowning out everything.

As suddenly as it had started, the downpour stopped. Ezra looked over his right shoulder to see a patch of blue sky widening in the west, and then looked behind him to see the band of ragged men stagger back to their positions in the line. He recognized some: Michael the pedlar, Bartholomew the drunk, the local tax collector, a long line of men just like him, all with crooked hearts.

It was Ezra's turn; he took a deep breath and stepped into the river. "Rabbi," he whispered, head lowered, struggling to keep from trembling, "I'm ready."

The Baptist stared blankly.

"I'm ready to be baptised."

It was as if the Baptist had suddenly forgotten why he was there, or what he was meant to do.

Enough of this, thought Ezra; he folded his arms across his chest and dropped to his knees. There! he thought. Done! But as the water splashed against his chest, a great wave of second thoughts engulfed him. What had he done? He was a fool to think he and the water could ever be reconciled!

Ezra panicked, and was ready to bolt, but before he could rise again, the Baptist pressed down on his shoulders and pronounced the sin-cleansing words.

Ezra could hear the fickle air bubbles escaping from his lips. And then, suddenly and gloriously, he was up, gasping, spitting out water, and reaching for the light.

The Baptist's large smiling face greeted him, but only for a moment, the look as transitory as the scudding clouds.

Ezra wiped away the water dripping from his eyebrows. "Rabbi, who was that man who came before me?" Prophets were busy men, and this one busier than most. Ezra was one of the many, and the Baptist had moved on. He seemed to have forgotten about Ezra completely, and was now looking out at the long line of sinners still waiting for immersion. Once again, he called out, his voice now more a croak than a yell:

> Prepare the way of the Lord;
> make his paths straight."[17]

Ezra was ready to join the others on the west bank. At the last moment, however, the Baptist grabbed him by the arm and pointed in the direction of an unremarkable, retreating figure. He was indistinguishable from the rest, except for the small band which had gathered around him.

Ezra stared at the retreating figure, then back at the Baptist, his gaze switching back and forth. "Ah!" Ezra cried. At last! It was the eyes! Finally he understood what it was about the Baptist's face that had so—he hardly had the words— that had so cut into his soul. The Baptist's eyes *burned*. That was it exactly! They *burned*. And now they turned one last time and seared into his. For a moment, Ezra could not breathe.

"The man you asked about—" With a trembling arm, the Baptist pointed to the retreating figure and the half dozen eager men surrounding him. "*He will baptise you with the Holy Spirit and with fire!*"[18]

Only Say the Word

The swirling sand pricked the devil's exposed cheeks. Still he trudged on, ignoring the protests of his camel. "Forward, you stupid beast!" he cried out.

Grit caked the camel's eyelashes, and dirty yellow froth bubbled from his lips.

"Stay then," the devil yelled. "It means nothing to me!"

The camel bent his legs, one at a time, then collapsed to the ground, burying his head against his chest. Better to become a living sand dune, his final groan seemed to say, than to endure the pull of a devil's rope.

Something caught the devil's eye. Barely discernible atop a small outcrop, stood what appeared to be a human figure. His erect posture seemed improbable. Was it another spirit like himself? Or a trick of the eye? Some strange rock formation that mimicked the human form?

The devil marched closer, his trailing footsteps almost immediately filling with sand. "You there!" the devil cried out, but the wind swallowed his syllables.

The devil increased his pace, now climbing a moderate slope. "What do you think you're doing?" His voice was a mix of contempt and delight. "Is it your wish to die up here?"

It might have been a rock sculpture after all, for the tall, thin figure still had not moved. His gaze seemed fixed upon something very distant. Finally he turned and met the devil's eye.

"Ah!" the devil exclaimed, "it is alive after all!"

For a long while, neither soul spoke. The devil sat and removed the wrapping from his face. From his pocket, he pulled out a portion of bread and cheese, and munched furiously. At regular intervals he spat out sand. "You don't eat?" the devil asked.

The man had large, sad eyes. His eyebrows, his beard, his shaggy hair—all of him—was thick with coarse sand.

"Come, come!" the devil said, inviting the man to sit beside him. He held out his hand, offering food.

The man sat.

"Look at you!" the devil said, "You're nothing but skin and bones!" The last word made the devil gag. He coughed, swore loudly, then spat out more sand. "Here, eat!"

Still the man said nothing; he simply blinked and brushed the hair away from his eyes. The devil thrust a hand out into the empty air, pre-empting any response "No, *don't tell me*, you are spirit and don't require food!" The devil laughed. "Is that it?"

More annoying than the wind was the creature's silence, but the devil was careful to hide his displeasure. "Or perhaps you are the Son of God whose angels will heed his smallest bidding!" *There was something about the man's face, something disturbingly familiar. Normally the devil was very good with faces, but THIS one. . . .*

"Am I right then? You're the Son of God?"

The wind stopped suddenly. For half a minute, the dust remained suspended, as if caught by surprise. Finally, the particles began their gentle descent, gradually revealing the dome of a pale blue sky.

Humph, thought the devil, earthly weather—as fickle as the human heart. The devil used his sleeve to brush clean the surface of some nearby stones.

"Well, that being the case . . ." The devil paused to remove grit from his teeth, then bowed in mock adoration. "The Son of Man could quite easily turn these stones into bread, or so I have heard." The devil's crooked smile resembled a fish hook. "Perhaps it is just an old wives' tale."

The devil could fake patience with the best of them, but in truth, the situation puzzled him. There was nothing special about the figure who sat before him; he was a man, no more, with all the frailties of any man, and yet one could never discount the trickery of the Creator who could hide behind the most humble of guises. "Well," said the devil, resuming his confident tone, "be my guest then; *command these stones to become loaves of bread.*"[19]

The man's dried and cracked lips opened. For a moment, it was not clear any words would come. Indeed the man's first words were weak and raspy, but strengthened as he continued: "*One does not live by bread alone.*"

"Ah!" the devil squealed, "it has a voice and can quote Scripture!"

"*But,*" continued the voice, "*by every word that comes from the mouth of God.*"[20]

"So you know God *personally*?" The devil was accustomed to yelling and rants, and to groveling and pleas, and even to the thrust of Greek logic, but the man's silence took him by surprise. Something new. But *really*, was anything ever, in fact, *new*?

"As a personal favor then, as one pilgrim to another, please—turn these stones into bread." The devil folded his hands, adopting his most conciliatory posture. "A very *small* miracle, a token, so I know I'm not wasting my time with some . . ." The devil scanned his surroundings, reminding himself of just where he was and in which era. "Some . . . goat-herding crackpot."

The devil raised a gourd to his mouth, drinking loudly and liberally. Water dribbled down his grizzled chin.

The devil belched and stood. He groaned sensuously, stretching out his arms. "We're a long way from Jerusalem, my friend!" The devil turned suddenly and grabbed the man by the armpits, lifting him to his feet. The man did not resist.

"Heavens, man, you really need to eat *something*. If you get any lighter, the wind will blow you away!" The devil thumped the man on the back, half expecting him to fall over, but he stumbled only a little.

The devil looked off into the distance, pointing: "*That* way, do you think?"

The man said nothing, only shielded his eyes from the sun.

"Jerusalem," the devil continued, his words as smooth as honey, and his head nodding like a connoisseur, "a very fine city. And the *Temple*!" Here the devil threw open his hands, ecstatic at the vision. "Is there any building like it? As a good Jew, no doubt you have seen it many times." Grinning, sighing slightly, the devil offered the man a drink, but he refused this also.

Unperturbed, the devil continued, "Sometimes, I like to imagine myself with wings—wouldn't that be something?" Again the devil thumped the man on the back. "And if I had wings, do you know what I would do?"

To the devil's delight, the man responded. "What?"

"Many things!" the devil replied, "but first, I would fly to the top of Jerusalem's temple. Stand upon its golden roof. From there, like a great eagle,

I would look over all the world and declare, 'Look at me! I am Lord of all that I can see!' "

Both figures paused. In the distance two jackals trotted by, focused on other urgent business, paying no attention to them.

"What about you?" the devil asked. "Can you imagine yourself atop the Temple? Lord of all Judea?" The devil paused, preparing a final thrust. "And you could just jump off, couldn't you? Wings or not. For God's angels would lift you up. Does Scripture not say this very thing?

> On their hands they will bear you up,
> so that you will not dash your foot against a stone."[21]

The devil stared hard into the man's face, looking for the least crack or hesitation. "How could you *not* do it?"

"Do what?"

"Jump, of course! Just to see! Because you could, couldn't you?" The devil reached out and lifted the man's chin, forcing an exchange of gazes. "Just for the sheer thrill of it!"

The man's expression was unchangeable: weary, stoic. Determined, maybe? The devil, who prided himself on being an expert in such matters, did not know how to read such a face.

In an even, controlled tone, the man finally replied, "*Again it is written, 'Do not put the Lord your God to the test.'* "[22]

Snorting and shaking his head, the devil looked away. "*Test*? What test? Who's testing? Is a man not meant to live? To breathe? To drink and eat and hold a woman in his arms?" Again the devil turned back to check. Was there perhaps just the tiniest tremor in the man's countenance?

"But you *have* held a woman in your arms, yes? And drunk sweet wine? And tasted of all Yahweh's great blessings?" The devil put his arm around the man's shoulder and squeezed. "Life's pleasures are fathomless, my friend. Such joy awaits a man like yourself. And it is all just there for the taking."

The man made no reply.

"Come, come," the devil said, again grabbing the man's arm and leading him closer to the cliff's edge. "Look there—beyond the farthest mountains. What lies beyond them, do you think?"

More silence.

"*Greater* mountains still. Mountains which make Horeb look like a mere bump. And cities beside which Jerusalem is a mere village. Golden, bejewelled temples and towers soaring up to the heavens. Wonders and entertainments that exceed men's dreams. Surely you can see it?" The devil looked directly into the man's eyes. "You are a man of exceptional vision; it is obvious to anyone."

Was he the Son of God, or was he not? Best to assume he was. The devil massaged the man's neck.

"So join me, my friend—a little imaginary foray—where's the harm? Picture the two of us on the world's tallest mountain. And there, spread out at our feet, are all the world's wonders and their custodians, merely waiting to do our bidding. You have only to ask, my friend. It is as easy as letting go." The devil laughed. It was a warm laugh, seductive. "Just let go. It is no harder than falling into a soft, warm bed, or into the perfumed hands of a hundred welcoming maidens. '*Ask and it will be given you*.'[23] Is this not so?"

The devil led the man to the very edge of the cliff. It was not a great drop, but it would do. At its bottom were the bones of three unfortunate sheep. "You have only to say the word, my friend, a mere word; it's that simple. Bow your head, or take a knee, your choice. Only say the word."

The devil inhaled deeply, as if gathering into his lungs all the world's material temptations. "But first things first, my friend, take a sip." He held out the succulent water gourd. Its wet skin glistened in the sun, water droplets clinging to its side. "Now I ask you—forget kingdoms and gold, mere baubles in the great scheme of things, am I right?—is there anything in this world, more welcome, more restorative, more to be desired, than a drink of good, clean, cold water?"

The devil winked. It was among his greatest weapons. "Please, I beg you. It would be a comfort to me."

The man stood silent and perfectly still.

"What harm can possibly come from one small sip?"

Time stood still as the devil's question hung in the air. They were painted figures in a painted landscape.

"No!" the man yelled, shattering the desert tableau. His one roaring syllable roused wind and sand and engulfed them in a great, angry cloud of dust. "*Away with you, Satan!*"[24] The man shook free his hand, and stepped away from the cliff and into the brunt of the coarse wind.

When the dust settled, the devil was gone. All that remained was a lone man still standing on a wind-polished outcrop, patiently brushing the sand from his clothes.

Below him, not that far away, a sand dune began to tremble. It startled the man, but then made him smile. The dune collapsed and revealed its true form—a forlorn and neglected camel.

"I'll be right there!" the man called out, walking quickly downhill—in the end, breaking into a trot. The man laughed to find securely fastened to the side of the camel's back a large bag of water. From another bag, the man pulled out a copper vessel, and into it poured half the bag of water, placing the vessel at the camel's feet.

"Drink, my brother!" the man said. The rest of the water, the man kept for himself, at first pouring it over over his bare head, then directing the final few gulps into his gaping mouth.

Man and beast drank loudly and sloppily, till finally the man wiped his mouth and asked: "Ready?"

The camel groaned; it was in his nature.

Laughing, the man pointed north. "Come, my friend. Our destiny awaits!"

Stolen Sons

Like the motion of his fishing boat, Zebedee's thoughts bobbed up and down, unable to rest in one place. Charlatan or prophet? It was hard to know *what* he thought of the man who had stolen his sons.

For a Galilean fisherman, Zebedee was doing well. He had *two* boats: one manned by his sons James and John, and the other by himself and two hired hands.

Zebedee shook his head as he looked at his hired help. Their faces were weather-beaten like his, their hands large, their conversation—what little there was—entirely predictable. If anything went on in their heads, Zebedee had seen no sign of it. Yet was this a liability? For a fisherman? Zebedee wasn't sure. All he *could* be sure of was that his sons were gone. Just like that. Might as well have been snatched up in the jaws of a whale.

"Zebedee!" one of the hired hands called out. "Maybe tomorrow the catch will be better!"

Zebedee looked toward the barely risen sun. How could the fish be there one night—in abundance—and the next night, not there at all? It was a question which had haunted him all his life—a mystery, his son John had called it.

John, John, John. . . . Just thinking of the boy's name made him sigh. Zebedee had hoped that hard, steady work would cure his son of his contemplative leanings, but it had not. "Keep your eye on the fish!" he would shout from the stern of the boat. Half the time, John didn't seem to hear; half the time he would just smile or whistle. No one in Zebedee's family whistled—only John—and, worse still, he would do it even on the water! Did the boy wish to bring bad luck upon the entire family?

The other hired hand slapped his friend on the shoulder and laughed triumphantly, as if making a great intellectual breakthrough. "Maybe Jesus caught all our fish!"

Four days ago, the catch had been unbelievable, *miraculous*, in John's words. But it hadn't started out that way; they'd fished all night and caught nothing. Dejected, Zebedee instructed his crews to head for shore. As usual, Simon and Andrew—friendly competitors—beat them to the task. It was always like this with Simon, less so with Andrew. Simon had to be first. First out, first in, always the one to catch the most fish. Except that that morning, his boat too was empty.

"What did you catch?" Andrew shouted out to Zebedee's boats.

"Nothing," James answered.

"Same here," Andrew replied, but already Andrew's attention was elsewhere, trying to locate his brother who was lost in the inexplicably large crowd which had assembled on the beach.

Zebedee couldn't say if it was Jesus who first approached Simon or the other way around, but soon the two men were deep in conversation. Next thing Zebedee knew, Jesus was standing at the prow of Simon's boat—his impromptu dais. Around the crescent of beach, the crowd huddled close, moving right to the water's edge. Crouched down like cats ready to spring, Zebedee's two hired hands looked pleadingly at their boss. "Go, go!" Zebedee said, waving a defeated hand. After all, there were no fish to clean; what attention the nets needed, Zebedee could manage by himself.

Very soon a hush fell upon the crowd. Small waves lapped against a pebbly shore. Otherwise it was quiet, but for a single voice. Zebedee was too distant to make out individual words, but he knew nonetheless that the voice was of unusual quality, riveting. No one coughed, no one stirred.

Zebedee was mending the last of the nets when Jesus finished. The noise of the crowd rose suddenly and many approached the boat and took Jesus's hand. Who *was* this man? Some kind of storyteller? Why had Zebedee—who knew everyone in town—never heard of him? Or maybe he was a merchant from some far off land Zebedee had never heard of. If so, then what was he selling?

Eventually the crowds dispersed and the beach cleared, including his hired help. Only Jesus remained, along with the four fishermen: Simon, Andrew, James and John.

What *now*? Zebedee asked himself, as he watched Simon and Andrew push their boat back into the water. They're going out *again*? What are they thinking? At least his own sons had better sense. They simply stood and watched as Simon's boat headed back out into deep water, only now with this mysterious stranger as passenger.

Simon was no fool. Zebedee could imagine full well his consternation. "With respect, Master, it's a waste of time. We've been out all night and caught nothing." Zebedee would have said as much himself, only not so politely.

And then—God knows why—Simon and Andrew threw their net overboard. Zebedee shaded his eyes with his hand and stared out into the brightly lit waters. Suddenly the sea was roiling, alive with fish. Even from this distance, Zebedee could hear the fishermen laughing. Back on the beach, his own sons were laughing too and pointing. So many fish! Andrew and Simon pulled and pulled—Jesus too—and still they could not lift the net.

To their credit, James and John wasted no time; they rowed out quickly to help. Straining to their utmost, the two crews finally managed to drag the bulging net out of the water—quickly dividing the fish so neither boat would capsize from the sheer weight of the catch. It *was* miraculous: the flashing fish, the rising sun, the laughing, the sweating, the boats loaded almost to the gunwales.

Maybe what Zebedee's hired hand had said was true. Maybe Jesus of Nazareth *had* fished the sea dry. Not only had the Nazarene taken all the *fish*, he'd snatched up his two sons as well.

Zebedee gritted his teeth as he thought back on that morning. He had seen it with his own eyes and still had trouble believing it: Simon and Andrew just *leaving the fish there*, still wriggling in the nets. Just leaving them! A month's worth! Off they go. Who knows where? Following a complete stranger! It did not surprise Zebedee that the hot-head *Simon* would do such a thing, but *Andrew*?

John and James did only slightly better, not leaving at once, but first returning to their father, albeit with idiot smiles on their faces. "Father," John said, "he told us he will make us fishers of men."

Zebedee shook his head. "What does that even mean?"

"I intend to find out, Father."

Humph, Zebedee thought; recalling the proverb about curiosity and cats.

James added, "You still have your hired hands."

And there they were, right on cue, back on the beach, no doubt curious about the commotion. Like children, Zebedee's hired hands were jumping up and down in excitement at the miraculous catch. Soon half of Bethsaida joined them, arriving with baskets and salt.

"And you can hire others if you need to, Father. After today, I think you can afford it."

"You can't just leave."

John put a hand over his father's. "Blessings of the Lord be upon you, Father."

And then Zebedee's two sons turned and began to walk away, never looking back. In a moment, they began to run.

And that's how it happened—Zebedee would tell the story many times—to whomever would listen—that is how Jesus of Nazareth stole the sons of Zebedee.

Three days had passed. Only God knew if his sons would ever return. Or the fish, for that matter. How could things change so suddenly? And why? It was unsettling and unfair. Let the sun rise and the sun set—that was Zebedee's motto. Let nets be cast and fish be caught. Let one day proceed like the next. And yet if what they said about the Nazarene were true—if one really *could* become a fisher of men. . . .

Zebedee turned to look at the shore where all this had happened just a few mornings earlier. In his mind's eye, he could see it still: Bethsaida's beach packed with people, like a school of beached fish waiting to be caught, or taught—maybe both words applied. And then Zebedee remembered something else John had said: "He told us not to be afraid." Zebedee remembered how this statement made him raise his eyebrows—easy words for a man to *say*. . . . "I don't want to be afraid anymore, Father."

A wave splashed against the side of the boat, waking Zebedee from his reverie. The waves had done this all evening, but only now did Zebedee notice them; he turned to his hired men and nodded. It was time to call it a day.

Zebedee stared hard at the empty beach as they made their slow but steady approach. He imagined the rabbi of Nazareth leaving imprints in the sand. He imagined the footprints of Simon and Andrew following close after, and those of his sons, James and John, not far behind. Finally, squinting harder, imagining more deeply, he saw *himself* on the beach also, thirty years younger, arms and legs pumping, kicking up sand in the faces of his laughing friends. "Last one to catch the Master is a scoundrel!"

A wave slapped against the boat's prow and splashed Zebedee in the face, breaking the sunlight into a thousand sparkling particles. Zebedee grunted and shaded his face from a cranky sun. "Fishers of men, my eye!"

Six Stone Jars

It was the day after the wedding, and a vulture turned lazily in a pale ochre sky.

"Take your time, Levi; what did you *actually* see?"

Levi sat in the shade, a nearly exhausted wine skin lying on his lap. He took a swig, then wiped his lips with a dirty sleeve. "I told you already."

When they were little, he and Malachi used to steal figs, tease girls, and swim in the creek, but now. . . . Well, things change; everyone knew that. Now Malachi was a Pharisee, and the things they were able to discuss together would make up a short list.

"You were at the wedding . . ."

Levi grunted, half-laughed. He looked down at his lap and watched his wine-skin jump as his abdomen flexed. "*Everyone* was at the wedding: Simon, Andrew, John, James, even *you*, Malachi."

"Why wouldn't I be at the wedding?"

Levi shrugged and shook his head.

"So then you notice Mary."

Of course Levi had noticed Mary. Who wouldn't have? Even at her age, with a full grown son, still she turned heads. Would you say she was beautiful? Desirable? It wasn't that exactly. It had more to do with the deep green color of her eyes—how they mesmerized a person. Levi brought his wine skin to his lips one final time. He squeezed hard to encourage the last few drops into his mouth.

"Yes, Malachi. As you said, I *noticed* Mary. Then one of the stewards came over and struck up a conversation."

"And?"

"Something about running out of wine—that's all I heard."

"Exactly how would that be Mary's problem?"

Levi shrugged. "Am I my brother's keeper? How would I know?"

Besides who *wouldn't* come over to Mary? Just to see those eyes. And when she smiled—well—then your heart would melt completely. Levi himself had spoken to her that evening, expressing his sorrow over Joseph's death—even though a full year had passed since. He asked about Jesus, how the carpentry business was doing and so forth; he couldn't remember much of what they'd talked about.

"Don't leave anything out, Levi. The details are important."

It was the calm of the man that got under Levi's skin. As if nothing could rattle him. Even as a boy, when they were stealing figs, it would always be Malachi who reassured the others they wouldn't be caught, that they had nothing to worry about. It was as if he had calculated every eventuality ahead of time.

"All right!" Levi shouted, rising unsteadily to his feet, needing the aid of a tree trunk to find his balance. "Here are your *details*, Mr. Pharisee! I'm looking over at Mary and she's nodding her head, smiling a little—you know that smile, Malachi."

"Go on."

"And then she calls across the courtyard to her son. And her voice isn't loud, but somehow it cuts through the crowd. 'Jesus,' she calls out."

"Jesus, son of Joseph?"

"Of course, Jesus, son of Joseph! Have you forgotten how we all used to steal figs together? Including yourself, Malachi." Except that when it came to the stealing part, Jesus would always find a reason to abstain; he would have to help his father or gather in the goats; it was annoying—the way he never complained about chores.

"I'm just checking your story for consistency."

"*Consistency?*" Furiously Levi grabbed his wineskin and flung it to the dirt. For some reason, he laughed after he did. Testing his balance one more time, Levi staggered across to the neighboring tree under which sat his inquisitor. He grabbed Malachi by the wrist. "Are you saying I'm telling lies?"

Calmly Malachi removed the hand from his wrist. "The best of us, Levi, can get our facts muddled."

"I know what I saw!"

"Which is exactly what I want you to tell me."

Levi sat heavily back on the ground, then shimmied his body around so that he sat knee-to-knee with this Pharisee, his one-time boyhood friend. Levi leaned forward, looking him directly in the eye. "Jesus comes over to Mary. And he has those same eyes, deep green, like his mother."

Malachi nodded.

"The two of them are talking together. And I can't hear everything they say, nor should I, right? But I can see Jesus with his head lowered. 'Mother, *my hour has not yet come.*'[25] That much I hear clearly. And they both look over at the wine jars, then at the stone water jars. Back and forth. By now, more stewards arrive, and they start talking to Mary, but I can't understand what they're saying because they're all talking at once."

"What did they say?"

For all his intelligence, Malachi was not a great listener. "They were all talking *at once*, Malachi, didn't I already say that? Except at the end, when Mary said to them, '*Do whatever he tells you.*'"[26]

"Meaning Jesus?"

"Yes!"

In his mind, Levi was re-living the scene, seeing mother and son locking eyes. In that moment, they seemed to exchange a whirlwind of secrets, and in Mary's eyes at least, Levi thought he could see the beginning of tears.

"So what does Jesus do next?"

"He speaks to the stewards."

"Right away?"

"First he—I don't know—just looks off into the distance, toward Gennesaret. Like he's checking for rain or something. You know that look he sometimes gets."

"And?"

Levi hated having to repeat himself. "Then he speaks to the three stewards, *like I said.*"

"And says what?"

Too quickly Levi rose to his feet. He had to grab his throbbing head. "How would *I* know!" In truth, Levi *thought* he'd heard Jesus say something about water, but it was a noisy place; he couldn't be sure. With such a head, he couldn't be sure about anything.

"Then just tell me what Jesus *did* next."

Still wobbly, Levi began to pace. "He just disappears. It was a big crowd."

Levi waited for Malachi's reply, but none came, which irritated Levi even more. "I've left nothing out! I saw only what a hundred other people saw! The stewards began to fill the six stone water jars."

"They filled them with *wine.*"

"I suppose."

"What else could it have been?"

Levi picked up a stone and hurled it as far as he could. He waited till the little cloud of dust subsided after the impact. "Maybe water! Who knows?"

"That's impossible."

"Who's to say what's possible?" Levi narrowed his eyes and glared at Malachi. He'd once seen Mary glare, back when Jesus was just a boy. It was such a look. It nailed one to the ground.

"Levi, you know very well that what we drank from those stone jars was wine."

"The *best* of wine! How could I forget?"

"So water never entered into it."

The family could never have afforded such a quantity of wine, nor wine of such quality. More than one person had said to Levi, and to others, to whomever would listen, "Usually they serve the best wine first. But here they keep it to the end!" Much drinking followed and much dancing. Admittedly no longer sober, Levi had glanced back at Mary and had seen how she held her son's hand. But it was just a glimpse. Wheeling dancers soon blocked his view, and when next Levi looked, they were gone.

When they were just young boys, they'd been throwing stones, seeing who could come closest to knocking pomegranates off trees, but then the game grew more challenging, and they targeted small birds, generally coming not even close in their aim. One lucky toss, however, found its mark, and the boys, five of them in all, gathered around the lifeless, feathered creature. One of them touched the still warm breast. Another spread apart its wings. All were amazed at how light the bird was. Finally, Jesus took the creature into his palms and walked back toward his house. "Where are you taking it?" Levi asked. Jesus turned and tilted his head, as if he didn't understand the question. Then Mary walked into the yard. Even from a distance, her expression made everyone freeze. Mary said nothing; she didn't need to. With large, searching eyes, she stared at her son, then at the other boys, then finally at the dead bird.

Smiling, Jesus looked up at his mother; he let out a tiny laugh, then threw open his hands, allowing the bird to fly up into a tree. It even sang.

"Levi," Malachi said, first needing to snap his fingers to get his friend's attention, "all this women's talk about miracles—it's just talk. You know that."

"You don't believe in miracles, Malachi?"

"In the days of Moses, of course, but *today*?" Malachi shrugged. He had not been one of the five boys throwing stones. "And *really*, turning water into wine?" Malachi's glare was nothing like Mary's or her son's; it was more of a smirk than a glare. "What kind of a miracle is *that*?"

Malachi stamped his feet, shaking the dust from his sandals. "What kind of messiah would be satisfied with something so commonplace?"

Crippled

Prophets came and prophets went. Behind every other rock, it seemed to Jacob, some wild-eyed Zealot was waiting to free his chosen people. Prophets even from *Galilee*, of all places! A land—at best—of half-breeds, fishermen, quasi-Hebrews, each one of them ignorant of the Law.

Why did these people not understand? The Torah made it crystal clear; Jacob and every good Hebrew knew these things from the time they could sit on their mother's knee: nothing must be added to the Lord's Holy Writ nor anything taken away.

What were they, if not people of the Law? The Law was *everything*—the sacred beating heart that sustained them in exile.

So who was this *Nazarene*—Jesus, son of a carpenter—walking about Capernaum as if he were Moses himself, performing so-called miracles, associating with all manner of sinners, behaving as though the Law did not apply to him? It had to be stopped.

Bad enough they should have to deal with the Romans, constantly be on their guard against Herod and his Hellenistic perversions, but now to be threatened from *within*!

"By the Holy Temple," Jacob muttered to himself, "just yesterday, did the man not dine with *tax-collectors*? What kind of prophet does this?"

Jacob's rant went no farther than his own hearing for, once again, the so-called rabbi from Nazareth had gathered a great crowd. It was infuriating; he had only to appear, and the people flocked to him—even a rumor of his coming was enough—and suddenly, like a plague of locusts, the peasants would descend, all too ready to be duped.

But hadn't his people always been like this? Too easily led astray by false promises. Jacob was as ready for the Messiah as the next man. *More* ready, for wasn't he a leader among his people? A learned scribe?

But not like this! The very idea was absurd—Israel's salvation coming from Galilee? From a band of fishermen led by a carpenter?

Again the great unwashed had gathered—before the house of one of the Nazarene's disciples. The rabble was thick and pushing forward. Gasps and cries added texture to the dull roar of their voices. It was as if some itinerant magician were performing tricks for them.

Already the crowd surrounding the house was five or six deep. There could be no hope of getting close at this point. Yet still they came. Jacob turned to see four men carrying a fifth on a mat.

"You'll never get through!" Jacob yelled.

Undeterred, they raced by Jacob, carrying their mat and patient to the outer ring of rabid onlookers. Finding no passage, they bounced off to another part of the crowd, trying there—again no success. They tried a third time and a fourth. Surely it was time to give up, but now one of the men began climbing the outside stairs to the roof.

What now? Jacob asked himself. He moved closer, not hesitating to push people aside.

A second man joined the first on the roof and spoke excitedly to his friends below. Jacob laughed darkly. It pained Jacob—how his people could be so deluded. But never did they lack commitment, though ill-directed, as it so often was. *They're going to enter by the roof, aren't they?*

It gave Jacob no pleasure to be right. Soon sticks, straw and mud were flying in the air. The crowd, initially hostile, now had a change of heart. They were urging the men on. They too had become admirers of the audacity. A dozen hands helped lift the cripple and his mat up the stairs and onto the roof. From somewhere in the crowd, two lengths of rope were found and these too were passed up.

Making full use of his status as scribe, Jacob finagled his way to the very front, coming within an arm's length of the Nazarene himself. Jacob was able to peer through the door and see the sky through the newly made gap in the roof. Now the men were lowering their friend to the ground. There were several close calls as the mat tipped to one side, then the other, and sometimes the mat dropped suddenly, only to be halted at the last moment, causing gasps from the few who could actually see what was going on.

Jacob stared in horrified fascination. So did scribes on either side of him, all there to bear witness to the Nazarene's misdeeds.

Finally, the crippled man and his mat safely reached the floor. His friends jumped down after him. Who knew what would happen next? There was no procedure for something like this. The Torah was utterly silent on such questions.

The Nazarene stepped back into the house and walked up to the man. A running commentary passed through the crowd, originating from the lucky few who could see inside. The men behind Jacob were elbowing each other and bringing fingers to their lips in a call for quiet.

The cripple's friends helped him sit up. He was dirty and sweating; it had been no small ordeal getting here. He wiped tears from his eyes.

Jesus said to him, "*Son, your sins are forgiven.*"[27]

The crowd remained silent, as if waiting for something more. What more could they want? Already this was too much.

"*Why does this fellow speak in this way?*" the scribe to Jacob's right asked.

"*It is blasphemy!*" the scribe on Jacob's left declared. Then he pulled on the top of his tunic, ripping it down the middle, visible testimony to the words of horror he had just heard.

Jacob followed suit, ripping his tunic as far as his navel: "*Who can forgive sins but God alone?*"

If the crowd had been waiting for something more, the moment had arrived. The scribes had caught the Nazarene in the very act of public blasphemy, and the consequences would be dire.

Jesus turned and asked, "*Why do you raise such questions in your hearts?*"[28]

Was this Galilean, the son of a carpenter, addressing *him* in particular? Defiantly, Jacob folded his arms across his chest. So be it, then.

The blasphemer continued: "*Which is easier, to say to the paralytic, 'Your sins are forgiven,' or to say, 'Stand up and take your mat and walk'?*"[29]

The words circulated throughout the excited crowd, which pushed closer, causing Jacob to stumble. "Watch where you're pushing!"

This Zealot knew how to work a crowd; this much Jacob must concede. When the babbling finally stopped, the Nazarene spoke again: "*So that you may know that the Son of Man has authority on earth to forgive sins . . .*"[30] He placed his hands on either side of the crippled man's head.

The scribes gasped. "He calls himself the Son of Man!"

The madman continued: "*I say to you, stand up.*"

Jacob *should* have covered his ears—like his fellow scribes—but the outrage mesmerized him and froze him in his tracks. Then the Nazarene took three steps toward the door and pointed. The crowd parted before him. Again he turned to the paralytic. *"Take your mat and go to your home."*[31]

The man did as instructed, his four friends following behind, stunned at first, but then laughing and slapping each other on the back. Quickly they passed through the door and into the bright sunshine. The crowd cheered, and began to break into song: several different, competing psalms, till finally they chose one above the others.

At the last moment, Jacob grabbed one of the cripple's friends by the shoulder and spun him around. "No singing!" he screamed. "This is no occasion for singing!"

The cripple's friend looked at Jacob as if he had just been spoken to in some unintelligible pagan language.

Jacob glared wildly at the man. "Don't you understand? This will undo everything!"

The cripple's friend grinned and shook his head—in infuriating *sympathy*—how dare he? He tossed Jacob one of the lengths of rope which they had used to lower the paralytic. Then, realizing what he was holding, Jacob flung the rope to the ground.

Meanwhile, the crowd sang:

> *The Lord opens the eyes of the blind.*
> *The Lord lifts up those who are bowed down;*
> *The Lord loves the righteous!*[32]

Jacob stomped home in a wordless fury.

Table of Sinners

Win a prize, get a promotion, find a treasure—hearing such good news, what man would not celebrate? It was the most natural thing in the world.

Looking down his long and finely carved cedar table, Matthew could hardly believe what he saw. Even yesterday, such a sight was unimaginable—before him sat the most prominent men in the district, some of them actual Romans, a couple of Greeks, fellow tax collectors, but most spectacularly of all, Jesus of Nazareth himself and his disciples. At *his* table. In *his* home.

"I didn't know you had it in you!" Lucas, the wine merchant remarked, drinking deeply from his bronze goblet. He held it up in a toast. "Did I not tell you, Matthew? Nothing accents a celebration like a good wine. And I sell only the best!" The two men clinked goblets and Matthew managed a smile which, despite his best efforts, inevitably slumped into a frown.

"You should throw parties more often, Matthew!" Then Lucas turned to the man beside him, once more clinking goblets. Wine spilled onto the table in a happy accompaniment to the general merriment.

Why shouldn't the wine merchant be enjoying himself? He was drinking his own wine and being paid for the privilege. Of course, it was how things were done. You scratch my back, I'll scratch yours. Among Matthew's tax collector friends (could he really call them friends?) this amounted to a sacred custom. They kept careful count of how much they collected and compared notes. You wanted to extract enough to appease the Romans, but not so much to provoke a popular rebellion. Always, one had to take into account the Temple Tax. And, of course, it was necessary and *expected* to pay yourself appropriately. Matthew enjoyed a certain satisfaction in getting the balance between these restraints just so.

Yet now, for the first time, Matthew's hard-earned smugness came under threat.

He knew well enough—had always known—how he was despised among his own community. Fellow Hebrews would walk on the other side of the street when they saw him coming. Sometimes they would spit on his shadow. In the beginning, he would try to explain: *SOMEONE has to collect the taxes—better a Hebrew than a Roman.* Other times he would argue: *I'm only an intermediary; the idea of taxation does not originate with me.*

He had long ago given up trying to justify himself. And if he had managed to accumulate a certain level of wealth in the meantime, was this not fair compensation for the daily disdain he was forced to endure?

This night, such arguments seemed flimsy. This very party he was throwing—even *it* seemed questionable. His whole life—every truism he had taken for granted—now seemed weak and vulnerable.

Matthew turned from his reverie and looked to the far end of the table where the Rabbi was waving him over. "Matthew!" he called out, then a second time, "Matthew, come!"

Matthew's thoughts flew back to earlier that morning—how memorable it had been—thrilling and confusing, both at the same time. Jesus had just healed a cripple and—needless to say—there was a great commotion: shouting, praises, arguments even. For some reason, a group of Pharisees seemed very upset by the whole business. Matthew wasn't all that pleased either; people who *should* have been at his table seeing to their taxes, deserted him en masse, joining the crowd that surrounded the Rabbi. Everyone was talking at once, many just trying to get close to the man, to touch his robe, kiss his sandals. And, if truth be told, if it hadn't been for his position of responsibility and the unruliness of the crowd, Matthew himself might have joined them.

But all that was just another case of pointless daydreaming. Many times he imagined his epitaph on a Roman stele: *Matthew, tax collector and dreamer.*

But then Jesus stepped out from the crowd and called him by name. There had to be plenty of Matthews around; the Rabbi couldn't possibly be speaking to *him.* Jesus called out again and headed straight for his table. "Matthew," he said for a third time, now in a whisper, "come with me."

The bag of silver coins Matthew had been holding clanged heavily on the table. He pushed back his chair, stood, and hastily brushed the dust off his garments.

His feet were unable to keep up with his thoughts; Matthew tripped and almost fell before finally standing beside Jesus and asking, "What can I do for you, Rabbi?"

Pharisee, Sadducee, and peasant Jew were all of one mind about this spectacle—Jesus of Nazareth, a prophet of Israel, standing there with his hand on the shoulder of a *tax collector*—it was scandalous, unthinkable! "Rabbi," Matthew remembered whispering, "your hand—you really shouldn't . . ."

Jesus's disciples must have been following close behind as the two of them walked together down the dusty street, but Matthew had no memory of it. What they spoke about, he had little recollection of either, except that Matthew—Heaven knows where he found the courage—invited the Rabbi to dine with him that evening. Matthew remembered how his heart leapt in his chest when Jesus accepted. How could all this be happening? And so quickly? So unexpectedly?

Once again, Matthew was being summoned—this time under his own roof. What could Jesus want? Was there something wrong with the food? Did he not like the wine?

The Rabbi and his disciples were seated at the table's far end. Matthew guessed they were more than happy to be far away from the "unclean" diners opposite. To be in Matthew's presence at all was enough to make them uncomfortable. And though Matthew couldn't discern their individual words, he had no trouble hearing the grumbles and noticing that one disciple refused to eat any food at all. On the other hand, the one named John gave Matthew a friendly greeting, and another, though he spoke gruffly and wouldn't look him in the eye, remarked at least that the food tasted good.

"You're most welcome—all of you!" Matthew said.

Grumbles continued to outnumber smiles. From the disciple called Judas came a derisive snort.

Jesus then made an extraordinary request; he asked Matthew permission to serve the wine—not to his own disciples—but particularly to the men at the opposite end of the table—who, in the eyes of any pious Hebrew, were clearly unclean.

"Of course," Matthew replied, stammering and wide-eyed as he slowly passed the ewer to Jesus.

Mouths agape, the disciples and Matthew watched as Jesus made his rounds, pouring wine, conversing, smiling, bending his head low to share a confidence.

"But they are Gentiles!" one of the disciples protested.

"Tax collectors!" said another.

Peter dropped his knife to his plate and its clanging echoed the general consternation.

Among his many gifts, Jesus seemed to have exceptional hearing , and he overheard these comments. He turned to Peter and tilted his head, as if in mild disappointment: "Peter, do you not understand? *Those who are well have no need of a physician.*"[33]

Peter grasped his goblet tightly. After a considerable pause—time perhaps in which to digest the Master's words—he slowly began to raise his goblet.

Matthew couldn't put his finger on it, but there was a certain quality about this particular disciple. . . . Matthew watched in fascination—a spectator frozen in time—wondering what would happen next.

Peter continued to raise his goblet, then stood. He turned to Matthew, looking his unclean host directly in the eye. "Blessings, brother," he said, his voice as gruff as canvas.

"Yes," Matthew answered, weak in the knees as Peter clinked goblets with him.

Gerasa

The merchant would not be easily put off; he scurried closer to his customer. "I can see you are a man of rare discernment, yes? You have the eyes of someone who has seen much—a world traveler, am I right?"

From the start, Philocrates had been wary of this wild-eyed merchant, so he had no qualms about cutting their meeting short. He sighed softly and began to fasten the straps on his mule.

"Bah!" the merchant continued. "These baubles and trinkets I showed you earlier—these are for *Galileans, Samaritans*, not for a man of the world such as yourself!"

He stood so close that Philocrates could smell the fish the man had eaten for breakfast.

"By the way, sir, if I may ask, how does a Greek come to speak such excellent Aramaic?"

Philocrates allowed himself a full grin, admiring the man's moxie. "I have many interests."

"You are a scholar, sir! Of this I have no doubt."

"Some might say so."

"Come, come," the merchant urged, waving Philocrates back into the shade of a palm grove. "I have something I'm sure will interest you. It is not something I show to just anyone." Out of his bag, he pulled a small box made of fine wood—Lebanese cedar possibly. Philocrates could only hope its contents were as promising as its exterior.

The merchant tapped the lid of the box with two fingers. Philocrates half-expected an incantation to follow and a smiling jinn to appear. The merchant leaned closer, speaking in a confidential whisper: "No doubt you've heard about the magician of Nazareth?"

Philocrates's eyes lit up, revealing an interest normally he'd have been at pains to conceal. But in the heat of the day, in the middle of nowhere, such restraint required more energy than he was willing to muster.

The merchant's grin revealed many missing teeth. "He was *here,* you know."

"In Gerasa?"

"Right where you are standing." The merchant pointed to his left. "And up there on that hill, our local graveyard." He continued to tap on his box, more rapidly now, as if attempting to deliver a coded message to an entity inside. "So clearly you've heard the story?"

"I've heard many stories."

"You are right, my friend! Our land is rich in stories!"

"*Rumors,* more than stories."

"*But,*" The merchant wagged a happy finger at Philocrates, "today is an auspicious day, for you have before you an *eye witness.* I was there. I saw everything."

Philocrates had heard so many stories, all unsubstantiated. If Jesus of Nazareth had done even half the things attributed to him—well, that truly would be something extraordinary. Philocrates chuckled, pretending to be more ignorant than he was. "Something about a man possessed with demons?"

"Absolutely correct, sir."

"And Jesus . . ." What would be the proper verb? "*Cast them out* or something?"

"Or something, yes."

It was difficult to decide which was more annoying: the man's tapping or his relentless smile. "And you *saw* this?"

The merchant squirmed slightly, less comfortable with a falsehood than Philocrates would have guessed.

"I saw the *aftermath.*" The merchant shook his head and stared at his feet. He sighed deeply. "And *such* an aftermath. . . ."

Philocrates lifted his eyes, pretending to search for a memory. "Oh, and there was something else—the possessed man's name was Lots."

"Exactly right, sir!"

"Because he had *lots* of demons in him." Philocrates smiled at the thought—it had all the makings of a folk tale.

"Lots and lots, indeed, sir. Hundreds I would think."

Philocrates chuckled. "If one could possibly count that sort of thing." The two men laughed together, sharing a fleeting moment of brotherly unity.

"And the possessed man was extremely violent, isn't that how the story goes? So they forced him to stay up in the local—"

"Graveyard," the merchant offered; he was working hard now to maintain his smile.

Philocrates pointed. "So what's in the box?"

The merchant inhaled deeply, struggling to regain his composure— Philocrates had no trouble imagining the man on an Athenian stage. "Well, sir, you'll remember what the demons said to Jesus?"

Among the many stories Philocrates had heard, this promised to be one of the more colorful. "You'll have to remind me."

"In fact, it was somewhat confusing; at one time there seemed to be many demons—at other times, just one. '*Jesus, Son of the Most High God,*' one of the demons shouted, '*what have you to do with me? I adjure you by God, do not torment me.*'[34] Of course, no one could *see* any actual demons— we saw only Benjamin, for that was the man's real name. As usual, Benjamin was foaming at the mouth, eyes rolled upwards, struggling in his chains."

"Chains?"

"Oh yes, we had to restrain him, day and night. He was like a wild lion, lashing out at everything, ripping off his clothes, toppling grave-stones." The pedlar pointed to a scar on his left cheek. "A souvenir from Benjamin—your Lots."

Philocrates paused, nodding his head, wishing he had parchment to record these details. "And where is this Benjamin now?"

It was as if the very name of the man put a bad taste in the mer-chant's mouth. "Who knows? Here and there. Telling his story to whom-ever will listen."

In the distance, Philocrates spied a small whirlwind. It was not an unusual phenomenon in these parts, but then he looked more closely. In the middle of the whirlwind, or perhaps walking just behind it, was a man dressed in the region's typical desert garb. There was something very odd about the man's gait, as though he were much lighter than a man could possibly be—as if that same whirlwind might easily lift him into the air. Philocrates turned back to the pedlar. "That wouldn't be him, by any chance?"

"No," the pedlar replied quickly. "Benjamin is not welcome here. Anywhere else in Decapolis, he may help himself, but here in Gerasa—what is it the Romans say? He is a *persona non grata*—Jesus too, for that matter."

Philocrates shook his head. "Surely if the man was once possessed, but now is cured, he would be something of celebrity? An attraction? People would make a special effort to come and speak with him?" This line of questioning obviously did not please the merchant, but Philocrates was insistent. "*Wouldn't* they?"

"Tell me, sir: what has Benjamin ever done for us? Apart from frightening our women and breaking our bones?"

"Through no fault of his own, surely? And after he had been cured . . . ?"

"But at what cost, sir?"

Philocrates frowned. "I seem to be missing some part of the story."

Tucking his box back into his bag, the merchant began to walk downhill toward the shore, toward Gennesaret, a lake they called a sea. "Come, come. You want the rest of the story; you shall have it."

It was a beautiful body of water, made all the more stunning by its contrast with the semi-arid hills. The shore itself was lined with oleander and fragrant jasmine, and a cool breeze drifted up into their faces. Just beyond the western horizon lay Galilee. Philocrates had even heard a story—the most unbelievable of them all—about how Jesus, the Nazarene, had quite recently *walked* across these waters—an impressive feat even for a Greek god!

The merchant brought them to the edge of a small cliff which abutted the sea. He bent over to pick up a stone and flung it into the water. "Thanks for nothing, Benjamin!" he cried out. He sat down, dangling his legs over the cliff edge. Philocrates joined him.

"Did you think I was always a pedlar?" He pointed behind him, toward the graveyard and hills. "I used to own land. I used to own *pigs*!" He picked up a second stone and threw it into the water too. "Then the Nazarene comes along. Not long after, Benjamin bursts on the scene, looking for someone new to torment." Another stone skipped across the water. " '*Send us among the pigs!*'[35] the demons cried out. Not just *any* pigs—*my* pigs.

"To be perfectly truthful, I was farther up the hill at the time—it was my hired hand with the pigs—but I could see the crowd, and figured Benjamin was up to his old tricks." Two more stones hit the water in quick succession. "Once again Benjamin was thrashing about; I could even hear his groans and yells—same old thing—when quite suddenly, all went quiet, which was

GERASA

unusual. Generally Benjamin's fits would last a good five minutes. But not this time. Everything grew calm: the wind, the pigs, everything."

The merchant threw his arms into the air. "Can you believe it? My life has been ruined by *demons!*" The pedlar turned and looked directly at Philocrates. "You're a Greek; maybe *you* know. Do such things really exist? I've always had my doubts, but then. . . ." It was curious to see the merchant at a loss for words. "Why *my* pigs? Can you tell me? And they don't just *run*—they *gallop*—straight over this cliff and into the water. The entire herd, all that investment, gone! Drowned! Just like that!" In his grief, the merchant pulled at a bunch of wild grass growing beside him.

Philocrates stared out across the peaceful blue body of water—idyllic, reminiscent of his home in Corinth. Only beneath *this* serene surface lay the corpses of many dozens of demon-possessed pigs.

"What was the *point?*" the merchant cried out. "He could have sent the demons into a pile of stones or a pack of rats—why my pigs?"

Both men stared at the gentle waves lapping upon the shore beneath them. Several small fishing boats were anchored offshore. Perhaps Jesus and his apostles sat in one. As miracles went, Philocrates thought, this one was very unusual—even for a Jewish holy man.

Slowly Philocrates rose to his feet. He put a hand on the merchant's shoulder. "I'm sorry for your loss." He began to walk back uphill.

"But wait, sir! You still haven't seen what's in the box." Beaming, the merchant opened it.

"What am I looking at?"

"Pigs' teeth!"

"What?"

"Teeth! From the very pigs that drowned in the sea! Demon teeth, my friend! Where are you likely to find demon teeth?"

Philocrates shook his head and smiled. "I think I can manage without them."

"But wait! Consider; it is the Son of God himself who is responsible for these teeth! Hold these in your hand, and it is as if you are holding a sacred souvenir from God in Heaven! The one true Jewish God!" Philocrates could see the merchant studying him, looking for a weakness, some final crack in that Greek armor that might ensure the merchant a sale. "I know what you're thinking, my friend, but I must tell you . . ." The merchant shook his head and tightened his lips. "He is a slippery character. If you are looking to meet Jesus personally, you may find that very difficult. *But,* if what you want is a genuine *artifact* from the Son of Man himself, look no further, sir!"

Philocrates hesitated. He knew it was the wrong thing to do.

"Have pity, sir, I have a wife and seven children; I have to salvage *something*."

Philocrates looked out over the water, trying to imagine the mysterious Nazarene striding across its surface. Was such a thing even remotely possible? The sun shone directly in the merchant's eyes, making him grin like a demon himself.

Or was that a grimace?

"How much?" Philocrates asked.

Unclean

"It's your turn, Thaddeus; *you* go back."

"Why me?"

Peter glared. "Because it's *your* turn."

"Besides," added Philip, "you are the fastest among us—a veritable zephyr. You'll catch up to us in no time."

Thaddeus realized there was little hope of changing Peter's mind—or the minds of any of them. "*What* am I to ask the Master again?" Peter began to growl. "No, wait!" Thaddeus answered, quick to deflect any criticism, "Don't tell me! I am to ask the Master if he wants us to look for an inn."

And then Thaddeus was off. Sprinting beneath the noonday sun.

The remaining eleven set off in the opposite direction, down a dusty road. "Why do you suppose the Master sent us on our own?" Andrew asked.

"To buy food," James answered. "Weren't you listening?"

"Yes, but why didn't he come *with* us?"

Peter laughed. "Don't tell me you're afraid, Andrew."

Andrew quickly glanced left and right. Jackals were known to prowl these hills. Lions, even. "This *is* Samaria—you never know what may happen."

This judgment evoked no laughter, only thoughtful silence. Why were they here in the first place? A pious Jew would go to great lengths to avoid Samaria—much preferring to traverse the longer and more tedious route along the Jordan. But the Master had insisted—almost as if he welcomed trouble.

They'd practically been chased out of the last town; they didn't need any more of that.

Judas coughed and spat on the ground. "Even the air is foul here."

Philip sniffed the air—as loudly as he could. "It seems fine to me, Judas."

"They are not even Jews, are they?" Judas's questions were almost always rhetorical, and when he was in a mood, there was little hope of changing his mind about anything.

John tried nonetheless: "They are followers of Moses, Judas, just like us. This is, after all, the land of Jacob."

"But they do not worship in Jerusalem!" Judas began to move his hands wildly and beads of sweat clung to his brow. "Great Father in Heaven, John, their holy mountain is Gerizim! *Gerizim!*" Again Judas spat between his feet, then ground his sandal over the unholy blob. "They make a mockery of the Law!"

"They are our brothers, Judas."

"*Brothers!*"

"And if they have lost their way, is it not our duty to help them find it again?"

His limp did not prevent Judas from surging several paces ahead, kicking at the ground and continuing to mutter to himself. For the next few minutes, the rest of the group walked in silence.

Finally, Matthew cleared his throat. "But John, isn't there some truth in what Judas says? I have heard many rabbis say as much."

John shrugged, then smiled. "You remember, of course, the Master's story about the good Samaritan?"

Matthew did remember; his head hurt with remembering—*so many stories, so much to understand.*

Thaddeus was still running hard when he spotted the Master. He was standing by a well—right out there in the open—beside a woman, a *Samaritan* woman. And, judging by her heavily painted face, a woman of questionable morals. Thaddeus skidded to a stop. Panting hard, he hid behind a sycamore and wondered what he should do next.

"When you're not sure what to do," Philip had once said to him, "do nothing."

Thaddeus had to put a hand to his beating heart. Jesus was *speaking* to the woman! Bad enough the apostles should be here at all—and if it were only a matter of passing through, Thaddeus could bear it—but for the Master to go out of his way to *speak* to the woman—and such a woman! Thaddeus doubted the others would even believe him when he told them.

It was midday, hot and windless. Thaddeus was grateful for the shade and the chance to collect his thoughts.

Now what? Could Thaddeus believe his ears? Did the Master just ask the woman to draw him a cup of water? Worse and worse!

The woman too seemed surprised. "*How is it that you, a Jew, ask a drink of me, a woman of Samaria?*"[36] Thaddeus dared a peek. The woman looked back over her shoulder, as if hoping for witnesses. "Surely, sir, you must know that Jews and Samaritans have nothing to do with each other?"

Good point! Thaddeus watched in horror as Jesus moved even closer to the woman. He could easily reach out and touch her. He was so close! Thaddeus had to look away.

"*If you knew the gift of God, and who it is that is saying to you, 'Give me a drink,' you would have asked him.*"

"I don't understand, sir."

"*And he would have given you living water.*"[37]

Slow down! Thaddeus wanted to shout. He wanted to remember every word. He knew John would want to know exactly what the Master had said.

Then the woman laughed. Too freely and carelessly as such women were known to do. "*Sir, you have no bucket, and the well is deep. Where do you get that living water?*"[38]

Thaddeus could help himself no longer. Even at the risk of revealing himself, he had to look more closely.

The woman was smiling, swaying, and causing the water jug to dance upon her hip. She spoke to the Master without the least stammer or hesitation, something Thaddeus had seldom managed to do. "*Are you greater than our ancestor Jacob, who gave us the well, and with his sons and his flocks drank from it?*"[39]

What a question!

There was puddle of water between them, so Jesus circled around to the other side of the well. Now he stood face-on to Thaddeus who had to duck away quickly to avoid being seen. "*Everyone who drinks of this water,*" said Jesus, "*will be thirsty again, but those who drink of the water that I will give them will never be thirsty. The water that I will give will become in them a spring of water gushing up to eternal life.*"[40]

Water of eternal life—Thaddeus whispered the words back to himself. He mustn't forget.

"Sir," the woman said—Thaddeus could not believe her boldness—were all Samaritans like this? "*Give me this water, so that I may never be thirsty.*"[41]

Where was John when Thaddeus so desperately needed him? It was *John* who should be hearing this, or Matthew—not him.

Jesus looked the woman directly in the eye. "*Go, call your husband, and come back.*"[42]

The Samaritan woman looked away. "*I have no husband.*"

Jesus nodded and kept looking at her, waiting for a response.

Thaddeus *knew* that look. The Master would not let this fish wriggle away from him. "*You are right in saying, 'I have no husband', for you have had five husbands, and the one you have now is not your husband. What you have said is true!*"[43]

The woman paused for only a moment, then dropped suddenly to her knees and kissed the Master's feet. "*Sir!*" she cried out. "*I see that you are a prophet.*"[44]

No apology, mind you. No confession or expression of remorse, just "I see you are a prophet!"

And then she spoke about the differences between her people and the Jews and how they worshipped on different mountains. But Jesus stopped her. "*The hour is coming,*" he said, "*when you will worship the Father neither on this mountain nor in Jerusalem.*"[45]

It was all too much, all coming too fast. Would Thaddeus remember even the half of it?

Jesus continued: "*The hour is coming, and is now here, when the true worshipers will worship the Father in spirit and truth.*"[46]

The woman put down her jug. Thaddeus could barely make out her whispered words. "*I know that the Messiah is coming. When he comes, he will proclaim all things to us.*"[47]

Jesus lifted his hand and rested it on the woman's shoulder. Unclean! Unclean! That Thaddeus should ever live to see the day!

"*I am he,*"[48] Jesus said to her.

It was at this moment that the other disciples caught up.

"Thaddeus?" Philip asked. "What are you doing hiding behind that tree? Did you give the Master our message?" Thaddeus began to stutter. Philip frowned and put his hands on his hips. "It wasn't a difficult task."

"But I . . ." All Thaddeus could manage was to point to the well where Jesus was still talking with the Samaritan woman.

Like Thaddeus, the apostles looked on in astonishment. Lepers were one thing, even tax collectors. But to consort with . . . It was unthinkable!

Thaddeus was no philosopher—not like John or James—so he had no expectation that he should understand everything Jesus said or did, but sometimes the Master asked too much of them. And it wasn't just him. He could see Judas pacing back and forth, and the others shaking their heads.

Finally, the woman departed and, at last, they could breathe.

"Master," Peter said, "we have food."

Jesus smiled, nodded, and waved them over to the well. "And I have water."

They moved as a group, happy, laughing, relieved, looking forward to a familiar meal among friends. Just as they assembled around the well and began to relax, Jesus suddenly stamped his right sandal into the middle of the muddy pool, sending a mighty splash in all directions.

Grinning widely, he declared to his friends: "There! Now we are *all* unclean!"

Roman Thunder

The sound was unmistakeable—eighty soldiers' boots marching in unison along a dirt road. When finally the soldiers entered town, it was as if a great bear's paw had pressed down on the main square, claws at the ready, and the blood-red cape of the unit's commander advertising to all that here was the world's premier killing machine, ready for duty.

At the prefect's whim, the Roman Army could appear at any time. "Looking for terrorists," a grim-faced centurion would generally announce, usually speaking Greek, very rarely a butchered Aramaic, words delivered by a man incapable of seeing that what he looked for could best be found in his own polished mirror.

Grinning, Andrew patted his colleague on the shoulder. "Ignore them, Judas. Just act as if everything were normal."

"Normal" was a word that Judas despised. For as long as he could remember "normal" had meant living under the thumb of the Roman Emperor; it had meant being taxed into economic and cultural submission; it had meant humiliation beyond a thinking man's endurance.

"But remember," his mother kept reminding him, "they let us go to the Temple. We still celebrate the Sabbath as we have always done." Judas could not help but think how much better a clean break would have been. Let the lines be clearly drawn between friend and foe. The so-called Roman "tolerance" was a fragile thing—kill a Roman soldier and see how far it would go. And now there was talk of the Romans insisting they worship their emperor! Can you imagine? Judas would die, would *kill*, before he would do such a thing!

"Come," Andrew said, laughing now, pulling on Judas's sleeve. "You know how the Master walks. We'll have to run hard to catch up!"

With one leg shorter than the other, it was no small thing for Judas to keep up—why did Jesus not take this into account? No, today Judas would not budge; he refused to hobble up the streets for the amusement of others.

Walking backwards, Andrew cried out, "Suit yourself, Judas, but I have no idea where we're headed. You'll have to solve that mystery for yourself." Andrew shrugged; Judas turned away.

Very suddenly the marching stopped. A great roar filled the air as one hundred and sixty feet stomped the dirt in unison, creating a cloud of dust that drifted for several seconds before settling on the sandals and bare toes of this multi-legged military beast.

Despite generations of occupation and years of well-practised accommodation, when the Roman Army stopped suddenly like this, every Jewish citizen stopped with them. Conversations froze in mid-sentence.

Judas thought back to the days of King David and King Solomon, a time when Israel too had an army, a *real* army, and bowed to no man. How he longed for the return of such days.

A snorting horse made its way through the phalanx. Atop the horse sat a centurion, his plumed bronze helmet reflecting the sun so powerfully that one could not look directly at him. Judas noticed him patting the neck of his horse, whispering to it, smiling, as if this creature meant infinitely more to him than any Jew or any assembly of Jews.

The clatter of hooves seemed unnaturally loud as the tanned and glittering centurion moved forward and scanned his surroundings; he was clearly dissatisfied. His horse echoed the sentiment with an indignant neigh. The centurion's heavily accented voice called out, "I am looking for Jesus of Nazareth."

Judas turned his head quickly, looking behind. Thanks to a small rise in the street, he had no trouble spotting the Master and his apostles. They were a few hundred paces away, almost out of town. They too stood frozen. "Go, go!" Judas whispered to himself. "While you can!" But still they didn't move. "For the love of God, Simon, get the Master out of there!"

As was too often the case, Jesus did the opposite of what was expected. Judas could see him turning, all too ready to answer the centurion's call. His reaction must have surprised the other apostles too because it took several seconds before they reversed direction and followed. They trotted to catch up, forming a wake behind their fast-walking and far too impulsive teacher.

"What's he doing?" Andrew asked, breathless, returning to Judas's side.

Judas answered with an immense shrug. "*You tell me*, Andrew. Prostitutes, tax collectors—what next? Why does he never listen?"

"He is the master, Judas. The pupil does not teach the master."

By now, the word had spread widely; heads were wagging, hands waving, and anticipation grew to a fevered pitch. What could a Roman centurion possibly want with Jesus of Nazareth?

"Isn't he . . . ?" Andrew tossed up his hands, searching for a name. "You know—the *good* centurion—the one who built a synagogue."

Judas sneered. "Honestly, Andrew, how can you be so naive?"

"I only know what I've heard."

"You hear what you want to hear."

"So I should be more realistic? Like you?"

It did not take long for Jesus to reach the town square. The throng surrounded the two men in an almost perfect semi-circle, making the space they occupied reminiscent of a Greek theater. "Capernaum!" Judas spat out the word. They had spent too much time here—it was far too Hellenized.

Jesus shaded his eyes and looked up. "I am the man you are looking for."

Much to the surprise of everyone, the centurion descended from his horse. Smiling, he brushed the dust off his shoulders, removed his helmet, and on foot, approached the man from Nazareth. Two servants rushed forward to hold the reins of his horse.

"Lord," the centurion said, "it is good that I have found you. *My servant is lying at home paralyzed, in terrible distress.*"[49] I thought if . . ." Here the centurion lowered his head and fell to one knee, his bronze greave digging into the dirt. The gesture was unprecedented; the Jewish onlookers gasped.

Judas pushed his way to the front of the gawkers, determined—*this* time—to miss nothing. It could well be that, among the apostles, only he would witness this exchange. This was so typical. They were never in the right place at the right time. They would miss half of what Jesus had to say. Samaria was a case in point—the woman at the well—so frustrating. And sometimes, what Jesus had to say was beyond understanding, even dangerous.

Smiling, Jesus put a hand on the centurion's shoulder. "*I will come and cure him.*"[50]

No!

Judas stiffened and grimaced as two soldiers lurched forward, swords drawn, but they immediately froze upon seeing the centurion's upraised hand and hearing his command to stand down.

"Master," the centurion said, slowly rising to his feet, "*I also am a man under authority, with soldiers under me; and I say to one, 'Go,' and he goes, and to another, 'Come,' and he comes, and to my slave, 'Do this,' and the slave does it.*[51] My word is all that is required."

The Master smiled at this remark, for reasons which left Judas perplexed.

Then this red-caped oppressor—bane of Judas and all his kin—*lowered* his eyes. A thousand times, Judas had seen this gesture, Jew to Roman, but never the reverse. "*Lord*," the centurion continued, still avoiding Jesus's gaze, "*I am not worthy to have you come under my roof.*"

Not worthy indeed—at least in *this*, the man spoke true.

"*But only speak the word, and my servant will be healed.*"[52]

As close as he stood, still Judas could not hear Jesus's whispered reply, though it was clear by the Master's gentle nod what it must have been. But *why*? And why *him*? Not only a Gentile, but a Roman soldier! Scum of the earth!

The centurion put his arm over the arm of Jesus, Roman style, and made his farewell. He spoke in Latin, a language which none of the apostles understood nor cared to learn.

The centurion marched smartly back to his troops. He mounted his horse, signalled to his troops. Erect and regal, he rode back through the phalanx. After a moment's pause, the second-in-command gave follow-up orders and the phalanx closed. One hundred and sixty legs turned and began to churn, a marvel of military symmetry. Very quickly they were a cloud of dust down the road.

Finally, the rest of Jesus's apostles caught up. "What just happened?" Peter asked.

"Nothing," Judas replied

"The centurion must have wanted *something*."

Judas strutted wildly, looking across the ground for a suitable stone. "If you were *that* concerned, Simon Peter, you should have been here. Heard for yourself!"

Grimacing slightly, Peter held out his large calloused hands, ready for reconciliation. "Judas, I mean no disrespect—"

"He wanted . . ." Judas was ready to explode, looking for a suitable lie. "*Directions!* All right, Simon? *Directions!* The usual! Another lost Roman!"

Eyes darting back and forth between the two men, Andrew did his best to defuse things. "It's what we *all* want, right Peter? Judas? Direction? What is it the Master says? We are like lost sheep, every one of us—sad, but true."

By this time, Jesus had rejoined them. It was uncanny the way he seemed able to sneak up, unnoticed. Putting his arm around Peter and Judas, Jesus smiled and gazed off into the distance. The sound of marching was now very faint. *"Truly I tell you, in no one in Israel have I found such faith."*[53]

Were these words meant to *shame them*?

Muttering, Judas began to limp away, needing his own space, needing to breathe! Why did no one understand?

At last he saw what he had been searching for. He thrust his good foot forward. There! The perfect stone for kicking to the very ends of the earth!

Two by Two

Philip was a heavy man, but not un-athletic. He walked erect and steady, and seemed proud of his well-trimmed, light brown beard. He scanned the landscape confidently, as if expecting to spot treasure. By contrast, Nathaniel's beard was black, unkempt, and wild—quite unlike his personality or voice. Mostly he kept his head bent low, and his eyes unfocused. Sometimes he would stumble over an unforgiving rock. "Philip? Why did the Master choose *us*?"

Philip made the road more unpleasant still by scuffing up a little cloud of dust into his friend's face. "In my case, Nathaniel, it was clearly because of my superior intellect."

Nathaniel waved the dust away from his face. "*Seriously* Philip."

"I *am* serious." Philip brought two hands to his chest. "After all, who among us speaks better Greek?"

Nathaniel shrugged; it was a weak argument.

"Speak Greek and you can go anywhere."

They'd been walking for hours. Their only companions were a distant herd of goats and the sun over their right shoulders. "Now, it's your turn, Nathaniel—confess. Why did the Master choose *you*?"

Nathaniel sighed. "Why would Jesus choose a nobody?"

"*That* could indeed be the reason."

"Because I'm a nobody?"

Philip patted his friend on the shoulder. "No threat to the Romans!"

All joking aside, Nathaniel knew there was some truth in this statement.

"Let's face it, Nathaniel: we're *all* nobodies: Simon, Andrew, James, John—all of us."

"Except Matthew."

"In *my* eyes, a tax collector is even less than a nobody." Philip spat on the ground. Whatever liquid he had added to the parched soil evaporated quickly. "But you're right, Matthew is a hard one to figure—and the moment people learn we have a *tax collector* in our group . . ."

"*Former* tax collector."

"Former or current, it makes no difference. This is not a stain you can just wash away. *Really*, if you had a choice, would *you* make friends with a tax collector? Would any of us?"

There was no arguing once Philip got started, so Nathaniel moved the topic along. "And then there's Judas." It was difficult to say the man's name and not sigh.

Philip scrunched his lips together. "Yes, our local hothead: a nobody who's determined to be a somebody. Good thing neither of us got paired with him."

"Puzzling choices."

"At least Judas is good with money."

Nathaniel laughed. "Which would be important if we *had* any!"

Again silence fell upon them. Both apostles gazed at the waning sun and picked up the pace. Nathaniel spoke finally: "I'm not sure we're meant to know."

"Know what?"

"Why we were chosen."

Philip shrugged. Then he smiled and raised his eyebrows, precursors to an attempt at humor. "The ways of the Master can be inscrutable!"

Nathaniel ignored the joke. "Remember that day you came running up to me, panting, all out of breath?"

"I try to suppress memories of unnecessary running."

" '*We have found him,*' you said. '*about whom Moses in the law and also the prophets wrote . . . Come and see!*'[54] Well, what choice did I have? Even though I half-suspected you were pulling my leg—as usual. But there he was, just as you said. He put his hand on my shoulder and whispered to me: '*Here is truly an Israelite in whom there is no deceit.*[55]. Welcome Nathaniel!' And then he looked into my eyes—such a look—like he had known me all my life. '*Where did you get to know me?*' I asked. Then the Master smiled—you know that smile he has—the one that makes you weak in the knees. And he said to me, '*I saw you under the fig tree before Philip called you.*' "[56]

"Why did you never tell me this?"

"He *saw* me, Philip. *Under the fig tree!* Even though we were separated by a hill."

"There were many fig trees. It may simply have been a lucky guess."

Nathaniel glared.

They walked on. Nathaniel kept thinking about how the day had started—
how excited the apostles had been: everyone smiling, nodding their heads,
just itching to get started. Philip was excited too—all of them, even Judas—
as Jesus gave them their final instructions, telling them to take only what
they needed for the journey: sandals, a staff, the clothes on their back, nothing more. An open heart would suffice.

"What about money?" Matthew had asked.

"Your Father in Heaven knows what you need, Matthew. Look for
some good person to take you in as his guest, and give him your blessing
when you leave. All will be well."

"How do we know what to say?"Andrew had asked.

"Say that *the Kingdom of Heaven has come near.*"[57]

There was something about those very words: *the Kingdom of Heaven
has come near.* They were like tiny bells ringing in Nathaniel's head. He mumbled the words to himself repeatedly, often not realizing he was doing so.

And that was it—no further preparation nor time to think or doubt.
Already the sun was an hour up, and Jesus divided them into pairs and
pointed them in six different directions.

"He really expects us to cast out demons?" Nathaniel wasn't sure
which apostle had whispered these words, but to his embarrassment, they
echoed his inner thoughts.

"Well," said Philip, putting his arm around Nathaniel, "ready to go
cure some lepers?"

Five or six hours had passed since they had set out; to Nathaniel it seemed
like weeks. What were the others doing? Had Simon—lately christened Peter—already raised someone from the dead? He wouldn't put it past him.
And how many lepers had James and John healed? How did one even *do*
that kind of thing?

Nathaniel thought back to a time in his youth when his father had
been very sick. "Nathaniel," his bed-ridden father had croaked, "Fetch
some water from Abraham's well. Then take it to the wise woman and have
her make me a poultice. " Nathaniel didn't know what a poultice was, nor
where in the village the wise woman lived. Nor was he even sure he was
strong enough to haul the bucket up from the well. It was horrible to be so
unsure about so many things! And yet off he went—running—but which

way? He went left first, then right, then left again. At each step his chest inflated like a bellows ready to burst. He was experiencing a very similar feeling now.

"Look," Philip said, pointing. "Can't be far now."

Nathaniel could see a few buildings—more as they walked closer. In addition to the bleating of goats and sheep, the cluck of chickens now joined the soundscape—and one thing more—a hoarse and pleading voice: "Have pity, sirs!"

"Ah!" Philip said, "our first beggar."

Seated beneath a fig tree, the man repeated his appeal, holding out a basket which he shook—not gently.

"I'm sorry, my friend." Philip showed his empty money pouch. "Before long, we may be begging there beside you."

Nathaniel grimaced and nodded in confirmation. "Not a single quadrans, I'm afraid."

Inside the beggar's basket sat two tarnished coins. "Much good the money would do me, in any case."

Nathaniel sensed there was a story here, and the beggar seemed determined to share it.

"Look at me," the man began, "completely useless. Once I was a baker, a *good* baker! Made bread for all the village. Now I can't even stand by an oven, let alone walk. I hitch a cart ride out here each morning and fight with the crows for whatever scraps passersby will share."

"You wish to walk?" It did not take Nathaniel long to second guess his choice of words. The sneer on the beggar's face only worsened his self-doubt.

"Of course I wish to walk! But that's *hardly likely*, is it?"

Of the two of them, it was generally Philip who was the more decisive; it was no different now. Calmly, he squatted down by the cripple, looking him straight in the eye. "My friend, have you heard of the healer, Jesus of Nazareth?"

"That would be the first time I've heard of anything good coming from *Nazareth*." The beggar spat on the ground, waiting to be contradicted. "So where is this healer of yours?"

"Good question!" Philip answered.

Nathaniel clarified, shrugging as he spoke: "Our rabbi is like the wind. Today he started off in Nazareth, but where he will end the day, only our Father in Heaven knows."

Grimly the beggar managed to grunt. "I could use a healer."

Nathaniel coughed into his hand, then looked at his partner whose eyes urged him on. "That's the thing, you see; we're followers of Jesus of Nazareth, and it's just possible—"

Philip smirked. "Possible is the operative word."

"It's *possible*," Nathaniel continued, "that we might be able to help."

With powerful arms, the beggar hauled his torso and useless legs a little closer to the two strangers. "How?" he asked.

Nathaniel threw a pleading look toward Philip, but received back nothing more than an unhelpful grin, and equally useless words: "I can hardly wait to hear what you're going to say next, Nathaniel."

Sighing, Nathaniel returned to the task: "It's *possible,* sir, that we may be able to act in Jesus's place."

There was a pause—long enough for a cawing crow to punctuate the thought emerging in the beggar's head. "You can make me *walk*?"

"Possibly."

"Can you or can't you?"

"We can try."

The beggar began to laugh. It was a long, almost hysterical, cry. "Go ahead. What harm can you do? Yahweh placed his curse on me long ago!"

Nathaniel recalled the many healings he had witnessed. The only trouble was, Jesus never seemed to do it the same way twice. Still, Nathaniel had to do *something*—perhaps some combination of the rituals he had seen.

He spat on the ground three times. He rolled the spit and dust into a paste and rubbed it between his hands, then began to lay those hands on the beggar's calves.

"What do you think you're doing?"

Nathaniel jumped back. "Sorry!" He began to stammer: "I thought this might work."

"Well clearly it hasn't!" The beggar began to wipe the disgusting paste off his legs.

"I have an idea," Philip said suddenly. He reached into his cloak for a small vial of olive oil—an item which Nathaniel had thought was forbidden—hadn't they been told to carry *nothing*?

"Oh!" said the beggar, his sarcasm rising to new heights, "now you're going to *anoint* me! I shall be King of the Cripples!"

Philip seemed unperturbed. "Better than spit."

Conceding the point, the beggar let Philip proceed. He began to rub the oil over the man's legs. He looked back at his friend. "I think this is the part where you say something."

Nathaniel's chest was burning. What should he say? When he *did* speak, the volume of his voice surprised even him: "*The Kingdom of God has come near!*"[58]

The beggar's amusement grew and grew. "Now, wouldn't that be nice!"

Nathaniel's next sentence seemed to come from thin air: "*In the name of Jesus Christ of Nazareth, stand up and walk.*"[59]

No one spoke for several seconds. Finally, Philip put the cork back in his vial. Two crows cawed in the distance.

"Is that *it* then?" the beggar asked, scoffing. "I can walk now?" Vitriol rose from deep in his chest. "Off with you two charlatans! Wasting my time! A couple of coins would have been helpful, but *no*, instead I had to put up with your ridiculous antics! Go! Go!"

Philips and Nathaniel rose to their feet.

"Sorry," Nathaniel said, "we really thought . . . Our master—"

"I'd chase you myself if I could!"

The apostles wasted no time resuming their journey. Soon the man and the fig tree under which he sat were distant bumps on the horizon. Then came an unexpected cry. Far off, but insistent.

"Sweet Lord in Heaven!"

The apostles turned. Was this the same man they had just spoken with? Who now seemed to be *dancing* under the fig tree?

"What did he say?" Andrew asked.

"I can walk!" the beggar cried even more loudly. "I can feel my legs! I can even run! Look!" And then he began to run, with considerable speed, leaving a trail of dust behind as he approached the startled and breathless apostles.

The beggar fell to his knees and clutched the legs of his benefactors. "Tell me what I must do! How do I thank this rabbi of yours?"

Nathaniel mumbled, unsure what to say next. "Well, for now, just follow us. We should meet up with the Master soon."

"Splendid! Yes! I will follow your Jesus of Nazareth to the ends of the earth! Just try and stop me!" The one-time beggar, now evangelized, linked arms with his two saviors and pulled them toward the center of town. Windows and doors popped open before them, and everyone came to see what the fuss was about.

"Look, everyone! See what these men have done!"

"Actually," Nathaniel whispered, "it wasn't *us*."

Grabbing his new best friends by the arm, he displayed them before the town like prized trophies; he was unable, however, to remember their names.

"Philip," Philip said, nodding and smiling. He put his arm around Nathaniel. "And my trusty sidekick, Nathaniel."

There was cheering and gasps, singing and laughter, and confusion mixed equally with celebration. Never had Nathaniel felt more out of his depth. Wide-eyed, he turned to his more confident companion. "So what now?"

Philip laughed and shook his head. "Not the slightest idea!"

Star Gazer

A refreshing evening breeze made the blades of grass tickle Nathaniel's ears as he lay on the hillside, staring up. They had nothing, and nowhere to call home—it seemed this was all part of being an apostle. Yet despite this, maybe *because* of this, Nathaniel was uncommonly content. He could not remember a time when he'd slept better.

What was it Jesus had said to them just the day before? "*Do not worry about your life, what you will eat or what you will drink, or about your body, what you will wear. Is not life more than food, and the body more than clothing?*"[60]

Nathaniel recalled a few snickers after this comment, but mostly the apostles were like him—hearing their master teach, their eyes opened wide and their hearts caught fire.

"*Look at the birds of the air: they neither sow nor reap*[61] . . . or *consider the lilies of the field. . . . I tell you, even Solomon in all his glory was not clothed like one of these.*"[62]

Yes, Nathaniel thought, it had been a wonderful day. They were all wonderful. Not *easy*, but filled to the brim with surprise and delight. And now it was night, and they could rest their heads and weary legs.

Above Nathaniel hung the Lord's holy firmament. It was like a rich velvet robe, peppered with tiny holes through which the celestial fires shone. The sight gave Nathaniel great comfort, though he did not know why. The night sky just *was*. Though curious by nature, till this moment, Nathaniel had never asked himself *why* the firmament made him feel this way.

"Beautiful, aren't they?" he remarked to no one in particular.

"What?" Philip asked, half-asleep.

"The stars."

"You're saying the stars are beautiful?"

"Yes."

Philip sat up and shook his shaggy head; it had been a long day for all of them. "Beautiful like a woman?"

Nathaniel frowned. "*No*, not like a woman, like *themselves*. Beautiful in their own way."

"Ah," Philip replied, in his confident (if not dismissive) voice. "That could be said of anything, couldn't it? This stone is beautiful, *in its own way*. This lizard, the most beautiful creature I have ever seen, *in its own way*. This crack in the wall—"

"How would *you* describe them?"

Philip shrugged. "Sparkly? Eternal? Why do we need to call them anything?" Philip leaned closer to his friend. "You're not turning into a *poet*, are you?"

Both men laughed, and their voices echoed over the grassy hill as all twelve apostles, most of them flat on their back, themselves looked up, each perhaps asking what word they would assign to the starry firmament.

"They are God's tools," Peter said, pointing to the northwest where the constellation the Greeks called the Great Bear hung just above the horizon.

Some called Peter the Great Blunderer because of his habit of jumping into things without thinking first (the opposite of what Philip would do, or *most* of them, for that matter). But Nathaniel admired the man's fearlessness. Make a mistake and just try again. Nothing deterred him.

To Nathaniel, it had always been obvious why Peter was the leader among them. This was not so to everyone—not to Judas, for example. As usual, Judas sat by himself, thinking—who knew about what?

Peter continued: "Every good fisherman knows Mezarim and how it points north. Every night, it guides us back to shore."

"Except," Philip whispered, "when the sky is cloudy."

"And there," Peter continued, undaunted, pointing due south, "God's great fish hook, to remind us of our duty."

Philip nodded, following Peter's finger. "The Greeks call it the Scorpion. You see how it has a curving tail and a stinger at the end?"

Peter considered, then shook his head. "Clearly it's a fish hook."

A cascade of voices began to debate—fish hook or scorpion? There was much laughter and pointing, but before long, only the sound of their own breathing remained. In the case of Thaddeus, it was more like a whistle.

"Thaddeus," Philip cried, "are you trying to wake the dead?"

"I can't help it."

"No doubt your wife was overjoyed when you left to become an apostle!"

More laughter, more pointing, but then a deeper silence. It wasn't only Thaddeus who had left behind a wife and family. For Nathaniel too, it was no easy thing abandoning everything he knew. Life was not easy. Every decision had a consequence.

"How far away are they, do you think?" Nathaniel gazed at one star in particular, quite close to the Fish Hook or Scorpion, just to the left of the bright red star which earlier Philip had called the Rival of Mars or Blood Star. But Nathaniel's star was pale yellow and, unlike its neighbors, its light was steady and un-twinkling. Why was it different from the others? "What do you think, Philip? Could a man walk to them?"

Philip grinned and shook his head. "No, my friend! The stars are *very* far away, but as to *how* far—no one knows."

"Not even the Greeks?"

"Not even the Babylonians!" Philip chuckled. No one else seemed to appreciate the joke, if that's what it was. "But I suppose the essential question is, can we *ever* know? Or maybe more important, should we ever *expect* to know?"

"Why all this fuss about little holes in the sky?" one of the apostles asked. But all Nathaniel could think about was Philip's question—how extraordinary! Should a man expect to know, *could* he know, the secrets of the universe? Why birds fly and men do not, where the sun goes at night, how far away the stars are! It made his heart pound just to formulate these questions. How he would *love* to know the answers!

Suddenly Jesus was between them, placing a mat upon the grass, then lying back on it.

"Master!" Nathaniel cried out, "we thought you were praying."

"I was." With hands still clasped behind his head, the Master turned to his apostle. "I still am."

Jesus spoke to them *as a group* all the time, but rarely had he come over to Nathaniel in particular.

"We were talking about the stars, Master."

"I heard."

Nathaniel laughed and let his hands flutter nervously between him and the sky. "I don't know why, but suddenly my head is filled with questions: is it the stars themselves that move or is it the sky that carries the stars with it? And how far away are they? What are they made of? Why are the stars even there?"

Andrew answered, "The sun is there to light our way by day, and the moon to guide us by night."

Quietly the other apostles had moved closer, surrounding Nathaniel and the Master, eager to eavesdrop on this exchange.

Nathaniel paused to allow the Master to reply (or even Philip, for that matter) but, when neither did, Nathaniel took up the slack: "What Andrew says is true, of course, but there must be more to it than that. Wouldn't you say, Master?"

"Yes, Nathaniel," Jesus replied, smiling broadly, still looking up, "I think there is more to it than that."

It was the closest thing to a conversation that Nathaniel had had with the Master in a very long time. It was quite wonderful. Dizzy with delight, Nathaniel turned his attention back to the heavens where the array of stars reminded him of lilies in a field. Or perhaps leaves on a tree. Or stones on a beach. Or—one could imagine any number of comparisons. Nathaniel was overwhelmed by a sudden awareness of the Creator's diversity and abundance. How much Nathaniel loved both these things. Why was there *so much*?

Hardly able to contain himself, Nathaniel grabbed Jesus by his wrist. "Is it wrong, Master, to ask such questions?"

Still smiling, the Master shook his head.

"Does it seem crazy to want to know such things?"

"Completely crazy," Peter answered. Most of the others signaled their agreement, but not Judas. He unexpectedly threw his support Nathaniel's way. "It's not crazy at all," he said, looking straight above him as he spoke.

Some were afraid of Judas, but not Peter. "What are you looking at, Judas?"

Directly above them sat a grouping of stars which the Greeks called Cygnus. "The Swan," Philip explained, pointing, "You see? With its long neck and short tail?" Nathaniel had no trouble imagining the swan, but he thought it looked more like a cross—a crucifix, to be exact. He shivered at the image and chased it from his mind.

"I am an ignorant man, Master, but I thirst to know the truth of things: the stars, how far away they are, everything! I can't help it!"

Jesus leaned over and whispered so that only Nathaniel could hear. "Be happy, Nathaniel, for that is what your Father in Heaven is: truth and love." The Master squeezed Nathaniel's forearm. "*Knock and the door will be opened to you.*"[63]

Bartimaeus

Someone had a drum, another a tambourine. Little children and dogs ran along the roadside, the children yelling, the dogs barking, and both kicking up dust. It was not even Purim, nor any holy day on the calendar, yet a festive mood filled the air. In this outlying slum of Jericho, the people grabbed with two hands the least excuse for a celebration.

"What is it?" the blind beggar asked.

"Nothing," Ethan answered.

Ethan wasn't really a *friend*. In fact, Bartimaeus had no *real* friends, only acquaintances. They put up with him, regarded him as something of a clown but, when push came to shove, Bartimaeus had no illusions about his status.

Could Bartimaeus blame them? After all, he was cursed of God, blind, a burden to his father and, really, no good to anyone. Yet he was not stupid. He *heard* things and understood them. He knew better than most when people were lying to him.

"Ethan!" he insisted, "tell me what you see. Who is coming down the road?"

Ethan pretended not to hear, a ridiculous pretence which only made Bartimaeus yell all the louder. "*Tell* me, Ethan!"

"A dozen or so men walking fast—like they're late for something. And at the front of them, a rabbi, it looks like." (There was singing too, hymns—not especially tuneful, but delivered with fervor.) "They're not much to look at, Bartimaeus. Farmers, fishermen, tradesmen at best—in a crowd, you'd never be able to pick them out. Hard to understand what all the fuss is about."

"But *who* are they?"

Ethan sighed and shrugged. Bartimaeus could actually *hear* the shrug, the subtle wrinkling of fabric and an almost inaudible rubbing of bones in the shoulders.

"Hail, Son of David!" a voice cried out. It had come from the farthest point in the crowd, beyond the hearing of most, but not that of Bartimaeus.

"Father!" Bartimaeus cried out, "is it the Nazarene?"

Timaeus (Bartimaeus's father) was a good man, so it was a mystery why his son should be so afflicted. Although widowed for many years, Timaeus remained in good health, and was renowned for his sharp vision, even though he was now in his fifties. His hearing, however, was another story. Lately it had deteriorated noticeably—which was a relief to many—evidence, at last, of some great sin in Timaeus's past.

Bartimaeus and Timaeus made a fine pair—comic to many—stumbling along the road together, their conversations shouted aloud for all to hear.

"It may well be the Nazarene, my son. I heard he might be passing this way."

"What Nazarene?" Ethan asked.

Timaeus put his hand behind his ear "What did your friend just say?"

The occasions were few when Bartimaeus could instruct others. "You need to shout, Ethan."

"WHO IS THIS NAZARENE YOU'RE TALKING ABOUT?"

"Ah!" Timaeus answered, nodding, "Jesus of Nazareth, son of Joseph. A very fine rabbi they tell me."

Ethan snorted. "Never heard of him."

But Bartimaeus had. . . .

> *The eyes of the blind shall be opened,*
> *and the ears of the deaf unstopped.*[64]

"And not just a rabbi, Father! A great prophet!"

"A prophet?" Ethan asked, his voice filled with unexpected loathing. "Too many of those around."

Singing and general cheering filled the air, along with the sound of tambourine and cymbal, (even rocks banging rocks when nothing else was at hand). "Jesus!" the voices cried out, tumbling and echoing against the stones. Sandals scuffed against the packed dirt, limbs rubbed against one another; there were gasps and groans, curses and praises, and a great jostling to get a better view.

"Is it him?" Bartimaeus asked.

"I believe so, my son."

The blind beggar rose to his feet too quickly, knocking over his basket of coins and momentarily losing his balance.

"What are you *doing*?" Ethan asked. Already Bartimaeus had stepped past him, stumbling headlong into the mob.

"*Son of David,*" Bartimaeus cried out, "*have mercy on me!*"[65]

A woman laughed and called out, "It's just Bartimaeus."

"What are you up to now, bothering the prophet?" a man asked, emphasizing his disgust with a hard shove to the beggar's back.

The woman spoke again, as she might to a small child: "Now, now, Bartimaeus, the rabbi isn't here to attend to blind beggars."

The mob manhandled Bartimaeus as if he were a stuffed doll, spinning him, tossing him, till finally he fell from dizziness. All the louder he called out, "*Son of David, have mercy on me!*"

The procession came to a halt, and the singing and percussion stopped. Everyone wanted to hear what the rabbi would say.

"*Call him here,*" Jesus said. His voice was steady and strong, cutting through the dusty air.

With Jesus's command, the mood changed. The slums of Jericho were often like this. The crowd could change from friend to foe in a heartbeat. Now a man took Bartimaeus by the arm, helped him to his feet, and gently led him forward. The crowd made room.

One man patted Bartimaeus on the back. "*Take heart; get up; he is calling you.*"[66]

"Come," Jesus repeated. It was no mere voice, but the sun shining. Bartimaeus threw off his coat and began to run, confident that the way before him would be clear.

He stopped just before Jesus's feet, sensing his presence without ever seeing him.

"Tell me, my friend, *what do you want me to do for you?*"

Never in his life had someone asked this of Bartimaeus, not in this way, not as if an infinite range of possibilities lay open to him. The blind beggar could hear himself breathing, could feel the beads of sweat slide down his temples, could smell the staleness of his tunic, the dust on his sandals, and the mix of perfume and dung in the crowd that encircled him.

A lone crow flew overhead, cawing three times, perplexed by this circle of expectant flesh.

"*My teacher!*" Bartimaeus shouted—for shouting was the gift God had given him—"*let me see again.*"[67]

Jesus touched the man's eyes—a transfer of lightning and life and light—making Bartimaeus cry out in a language no one knew.

"Go, Bartimaeus," Jesus said, "*your faith has made you well.*"[68]

Bartimaeus stood and saw blue, not knowing what blue was except that it was good. He saw black too, and it soared above him and cawed. All around him were bright shapes and a blaze of movement.

Jesus moved on, his disciples and happy onlookers, following.

"Bartimaeus!" a feeble voice called out.

Could it be? Was this his father? Stooped and shrivelled? Bartimaeus inhaled in surprise and wonder. So *this* is what old looked like. . . .

Bartimaeus ran to his father, embraced him and kissed him on the cheek. He laughed, picked up his coat and then, twirling, *almost dancing*, raced down the road. Faster and faster—Bartimaeus did not simply run, he flew! Soared like a dark bird in a blue sky. "Master!" he shouted (in a voice as wide as all color), "Son of David! Wait for me!"

For a brief moment, Bartimaeus paused and looked back at his father. Eyes full of regret and joy, Bartimaeus resumed his running.

Tempest

Peter marched toward the setting sun, veered sharply right, then left. He could not keep still.

"Sit *down*, Simon! You're making the rest of us nervous."

Andrew felt a need to defend his brother and the name the Master had given him. "Actually, Philip, it's *Peter*, remember?"

Philip rolled his eyes.

In truth, Andrew was as nervous as the others, and would have been on his feet too, pacing along with Peter, if he'd thought it would do any good.

Again Philip cried out, "Good thing you weren't stomping about like that in the boat or you'd have drowned the bunch of us!"

Yet they *hadn't* drowned. And now the six of them sat safely on shore (five, if you didn't count Peter, who was still pacing). They were staring into maybe the most beautiful sunset Andrew had ever seen. A few crimson clouds, looking like slender, languorous fingers, hung above the western horizon. The air was calm, the temperature pleasant, and the scent of jasmine was in the air. Andrew had to fight against an overwhelming desire to lie down and sleep.

Philip turned to Nathaniel. "I notice Thomas is missing. Typical."

Half of Jesus's disciples were always missing. It was difficult to keep up. From one day to the next, the Master would head off in a new direction, and you could never predict where it would be. At least Andrew could not. Across Gennesaret, then back again, around the sea, off to Jerusalem, detour to Samaria—you just never knew what to expect.

Unless you kept your eye on the Master every waking moment, you could very easily fall behind. As Thomas so often seemed to do. Andrew suspected it was intentional.

What was it a young man had said to Jesus only yesterday? "Teacher! I will follow you anywhere! I am ready for anything!" *If only he knew!* thought Andrew. Jesus had paused before answering: "*Foxes have holes, and birds of the air have nests; but the Son of Man has nowhere to lay his head.*"[69]

Andrew remembered how the young man's smile had faded, how his mouth began to droop, and how he had slowly turned and slunk away. *Good,* Andrew remembered thinking—almost immediately ashamed of his unkind thought—*one less disciple for us to worry about.*

Another time, a man with flaming red hair and a thick accent, had asked the same thing; he declared he was ready to give up everything and follow Jesus. Only let him first bury his father. Jesus smiled and held out his hand. "*Let the dead bury their own dead.*"[70]

It was not always easy to understand what Jesus meant. Andrew shook his head at the memory of these harsh words. Could the Master really object to a son burying his father?

Looking for some reassurance in the familiar, Andrew took a quick look around him, counting one more time: Philip was closest, right beside him. On his right were James and John, and to his left sat Nathaniel and Peter (Peter had finally settled down). That made six—seven, counting Jesus.

It amazed Andrew still—how calm it was. Unusual for Galilee. Not a breath of air. Whereas half an hour before, they were in the midst of a raging storm, and great waves had tossed their boat up and down as if it were a child's toy. Andrew had been certain they were about to die. And stupidly, he had just sat there, hugging the side of the boat, feeling the vomit rise in his throat.

"Lord, save us!" That had been their cry. It was all Andrew could manage to turn his head and see Jesus still fast asleep in the bow. How could anyone sleep in such a tempest? And yet (only now did Andrew reflect on this) how often *had* he seen Jesus actually asleep? Usually the Master was the first up, and the last to lay down his head; it was as if every single waking moment were precious.

It was Peter who finally grabbed him by the arm, shaking him. "*Teacher,*" he cried, "*do you not care that we are perishing?*"[71] A large wave lifted the prow of the boat, and Jesus looked down on them as he spoke: "*Why are you afraid? Have you still no faith?*"[72]

The wave crested, and a great wall of water slammed into the boat, throwing Jesus into the middle where a dozen arms caught him. With Peter's help, Jesus rose to his feet. He wiped the water from his forehead, smiled, then turned away from the disciples and faced the wind.

"Moses!" John remarked, as Jesus stretched out both arms. Jesus turned briefly and replied to John, but the words were lost in the wind.

In less than a minute, the wind abated and the clouds dispersed. Suddenly the sky was blue and—most mysteriously of all—the waves had vanished. This, none of them could explain. Always, after a great wind, the waves would persist for good long while, but not this day. The sea was like glass and the single sail on their mast completely limp. No one was able to speak until Peter shattered the silence: "Row! Row! If you ever want to reach the shore!"

All this had happened less than an hour before. They'd pulled the boat ashore and fallen to the ground, exhausted and laughing. Smiling, Jesus excused himself to go off to pray, but he wouldn't be long, he said. He headed west, walking quickly, as always—but easily. (Everyone knew Jesus was a great teacher, but how many knew he was a great walker?)

Still panting, their laughter gradually dying away, they watched as Jesus's silhouette grew smaller against the setting sun.

Suddenly Peter rose to his feet. "Who can tell me?" he asked.

"Why are you shouting, Peter?" James asked.

"Who among you can *tell me*?" Peter repeated.

Philip had never been afraid of Peter's gruff voice. "Tell you what?"

"Who this man *is*?" With limpid, searching eyes, Peter looked at each of them in turn. Andrew looked away, so did the others. More loudly, Peter asked again: "*Who then is this, that even the wind and the sea obey him?*[73] You all saw it! Someone tell me!"

Nothing pained Peter more than to have nothing to occupy his hands. Finally, he grabbed a nearby twig (likely not thick enough to satisfy his frustration, but it would have to do). He snapped it in half across his knee. He began walking—faster, then faster. "Words!" Peter growled. "Useless words!"

It did not seem to matter that night was falling and the sun now well below the horizon. Peter headed west regardless, as if he might still catch up to the sun's last rays.

Second Life

L azarus stopped in mid-plane, a curl of cedar wood standing erect like a crescent moon. He'd been working all day, past reason or need, just for something to do. And then he would stop, look at his fingers, wiggle them, look out across the valley and inhale deeply the lemon-scented air. The question would not leave him: why *him*?

Daniel came running—*running*—on a day hot enough to cook eggs on stone! Lazarus pretended not to notice.

"My friend!" Daniel's face looked like a shiny glazed plate ready to crack. "How *are* you?"

"I'm *fine*."

Lazarus hoped his supply of wood would get him through yet another unwanted conversation.

"It's a beautiful day!" Daniel stepped into the shade of the open workshop. The shadows of a hundred palm fronds fell on the dusty floor. Lazarus nodded toward a small table and nearby water jug.

Daniel picked up a cup, and filled it, and drank. Wiping his lips, he looked back at his long time friend, now the most famous man in Bethany. "Living water!" Daniel cried out.

Lazarus moved his arms back and forth across the length of wood in a steady and strong rhythm, as regular as a man breathing.

Many years ago Daniel had expressed a special interest in Lazarus's sister. It had been hopeless from the start. Neither family had sought a contract, and from the beginning, Martha had made it quite clear that she had no intention of marrying anyone. Ever.

Lazarus searched for another length of wood.

Bad enough to have one strong-willed sister, but Lazarus had two! Two who thought nothing of completely forgoing tradition and family loyalty and dedicating their lives to He-Who-Must-Not-Be-Named and who did not hand out dowries.

"Lazarus? Do you mind if I ask you a question?"

Angels of God; *here it comes.* Daniel had never been one to take a hint. Not even a great stack of rough hewn wood could save Lazarus. Defeated, he sat down heavily, and wiped his brow.

Daniel lowered his voice and leaned closer: "What was it like? Being dead?"

Lazarus noticed a tiny bit of blood oozing from a scrape on his knuckles. It was nothing. Still, from such a tiny wound, sometimes a man might die. Absurd. "My friend, you know as much about it as I do. You were there, right? So you tell *me.*"

Daniel laughed nervously. "Well, yes, we were all there. Family and friends from as far away as Jerusalem."

The crowds had come for the sake of Mary and Martha more than for him—Lazarus was under no illusion about that. And when word spread that Jesus might be there, the crowd swelled to nearly double its size. Or so the story went.

Daniel continued to speak in hushed tones: "What is it you want me to tell you, Lazarus? I only know that one moment you were dead, and the next moment you weren't. I saw you walk out of the tomb with my own eyes!"

"Ah!" Lazarus said, "an eye-witness!" Half-smiling, half-grimacing, Lazarus placed a hand on Daniel's arm. "How did I *seem*?" It was good to put the burden of inquiry on someone else for a change. "I have only my sisters' account, Daniel, and who is to say how reliable their testimony is?"

It was unheard of to disparage Mary or Martha. Haltingly, Daniel replied, "But your sisters are wonderful women. They would never speak falsely—"

"But they were *grieving*, yes?"

"For three days, wailing almost without stop! They were beyond reproach."

"So, through teary eyes, they might not always have seen things *clearly.*"

Slowly Daniel lifted his head toward the palm fronds; a gentle wind caused them to tremble. "Oh, I see what you mean—I think. . . ."

"You were there when Jesus arrived?"

"I was."

"And Martha was with him?"

Daniel took a moment to consider. "Yes. I'm almost certain she was."

"And what did they say?"

"Oh, Lazarus! Everyone knows the story!" Daniel looked puzzled—surprised, Lazarus guessed, to find *himself* the focus of interrogation. "Martha said to the Master, '*Lord, if you had been here, my brother would not have died.*' "[74]

"And then?"

Daniel took another sip from his cup. "And *then*, as everyone knows, Jesus asked that the stone be rolled away from your tomb." Daniel took a deep breath. "Of course, Martha *warned* Jesus. *That* much I heard clearly."

"That there would be a stench?"

"Exactly."

Lazarus could feel his face harden at the memory.

"I mean no offence, my friend, but that would normally be the case, wouldn't it? After four days?"

Lazarus looked away. He made a quick inventory of his tools, his limbs, the distant hazy hills, and finally looked back at Daniel who sat there with mouth open and eyes bulging. "And was there?" Lazarus asked.

"A stench? Well, obviously!" Daniel lowered his head, maybe looking for a way to rephrase his exclamation. "But it faded away very quickly—it was the strangest thing! Suddenly, all I could smell were lemons and jasmine!" Daniel turned away, looking out across the hills himself, as if needing to anchor his memory in a tangible landscape. "It must have taken a half a dozen men to roll away the stone—you can imagine, I'm sure. There was pushing and groaning—I thought they'd never move it—but finally, the stone began to budge—and once it got going. . . ." Daniel shook his head. "Amos managed to skip out of the way just in time—it was a close call!"

Lazarus put down his tools and took two steps closer to the shop entrance, gazing at the distant hills. Daniel handed him a cup of water, which he took with barely a glance, relying only on his sense of touch to wrap his fingers around the vessel's rough surface.

"It was such a scene, Lazarus! Everyone gasping and crying out, and some—forgive me, my friend—even holding their noses. Then Jesus explained that you were only asleep, and he was there to wake you. Such words, Lazarus! I will never forget them. The Master was calm as he spoke, smiling a little, but also seeming to fight to keep his eyelids open. Tired, I suppose, like the rest of us."

Lazarus continued to stare at the distant hills.

"Is that what it's like, Lazarus? Like you're sleeping?"

Lazarus said nothing.

"Do you remember *anything*?"

Lazarus moved his lips, but the words he uttered were only for himself.

Daniel leaned closer. "I beg your pardon?"

"I remember nothing!"

With great deliberation Lazarus inhaled—three deep breaths—as though only this deliberate action could keep him going. *He was sitting up; that was the first thing he remembered. Not where he was, nor even who he was. Just sitting up, surrounded by a warm, brown darkness. Slowly he realized his feet were touching the soft ground. And there was a voice in his head—no words, but a voice calling him by name, urging him up. Sleep was what Lazarus wanted most, just sleep. Yet he couldn't find his tongue, and that painfully insistent voice kept calling, making his feet stagger forward. The fuzzy brownness rocked him from side to side like a ship on a rough sea. Lazarus expected to fall and, if truth be told, welcomed the prospect. Still, the voice kept calling. His feet staggered on, and the brownness grew lighter, thinner. There was a crunching sound, stone pressing against stone. Finally, he heard voices, many voices. Too many—like a flock of frantic crows, pecking away at the brownness. The spinning and rocking was incessant and how bright it had suddenly become. And LOUD. If he knew where his ears were, he would have covered them.*

"You remember nothing at all?" Daniel asked.

In surprise more than pain, Lazarus screamed as his eyes, mouth, and ears—all were set free from their linen wrappings. "Lazarus is alive!" he heard people shouting. They cried out like mad roosters—over and over. . . .

Daniel sat hunched over, his forehead deeply furrowed. "Amazing! One moment you're dead, and next moment you're . . ."

A dozen arms grabbed him. His weeping sisters held on to his legs. Jesus himself came over, said nothing, led him to a banquet table, gave him some bread, poured some wine and reminded Lazarus what to do with them. "Eat," Jesus said, speaking with a fierce gentleness. "Like this," the Master said, bringing the bread to Lazarus's lips.

Lazarus stepped into the sunlight and raised his voice to full volume, still testing what he could do. "So tell me, Daniel—you've always been a great reader of books—what am I supposed to do *now*?"

"What do you mean?"

With a hardened smile, Lazarus turned to Daniel. "Now that I have a second life?"

Daniel stuttered. "Didn't Jesus tell you?

"He said nothing!" Again Lazarus turned away, inhaling so deeply the valley seemed to buckle. "Everyone looks at me, Daniel, just like you—the man raised from the dead! They wonder why *him*? Every day I ask myself the same question!" With a great exhalation, Lazarus let his breath refill the valley, restoring it "So now what? Am I expected to heal the sick? Change stones into bread?"

Roaring, Lazarus stretched his arms out to their full length, forming the shadow of a cross behind him. "What has he *done* to me, Daniel?"

The cry of Lazarus's broken voice echoed in the hills, causing crows to scatter and Daniel to jump up and spill his water.

Lazarus gripped his friend's arm tightly. "*He* should try coming back from the dead! See how *he* likes it!"

Antipas

Strictly speaking, what Herod Antipas sat upon wasn't a throne, for Antipas wasn't a king. *Ethnarch* some called him, *Tetrarch* others said, but what did it matter? These were mere labels, a convenience for Roman bureaucrats.

Herod Antipas belched softly as he surveyed his banquet room. He took much comfort in what he saw. His furnishings could match that of any eastern monarch. His cuisine was of the finest. Tonight they were eating gazelle *and* quail. A hundred servants were at his beck and call, and in the provinces of Galilee and Perea, Antipas's word stood as law, unless it happened to conflict with Roman edicts. He made sure it never did.

It was an art really: to be Roman but not *too* Roman. To appease the imperial powers enough to ensure their support, but not so much as to incite revolt among his subjects. Yes, thought Antipas, he was as much *artist* as king. And most particularly an "escape" artist, for it was no easy thing to be of the House of Herod and live long enough to reap the attendant rewards.

But Antipas *had* been patient—he had won the race.

"Dearest," his wife said, "was the dinner to your taste?"

"Very much," Antipas replied, eyeing his wife hungrily for she too was "very much to his taste." Who'd have thought he would make such a match? Herodias, a beauty, and smart too, ambitious. A queen truly worthy of him. And to think he had fashioned this loving coalition on only his second attempt. Without the interference of his father.

His first wife—well, what could one say? It was a well-intentioned political alliance. There was nothing wrong with Phasaelis per se—it did not grieve him to look at her—but when compared to Herodias . . . In fairness who *could* compare favorably with Herodias?

It's not as if he'd gone out of his way to pursue the woman. His intentions had been perfectly honorable. He'd traveled to Rome—never an easy trip—to visit his half-brother, Herod II. He was being sociable. Doing his familial duty. And it was there that he first met his brother's wife, the lovely Herodias. Eros did the rest.

It was no great thing to divorce a wife. His own father had done it many times. And as far as Herodias was concerned, she was quite blameless in the affair. It was true her husband still lived when she re-married, but only *for a short time*. And once *he* was out of the picture, what objection could there reasonably be in Antipas marrying the widow? It was a common enough practice—an act of compassion, really.

Regrettably, not all people saw it that way—people like John the Baptist, for example. *Especially* the Baptist.

Antipas had nothing against the man personally. As much as anyone, he enjoyed listening to him preach—John was a dynamic speaker. But was it really necessary that the Baptist take such a strict interpretation of the Law? *Flexibility. Accommodation.* These were the hallmarks of civilization. What business was it of the Baptist *whom* Antipas chose to marry?

"He must be silenced," Herodias had said to him. Repeatedly, almost daily.

"Yes, my sweet, but John is a prophet, beloved by his people."

"He besmears our reputation."

"But Herodias, reputation is a nebulous thing; it comes and goes."

Antipas sighed and drummed impatient fingers on the armrest of his throne. Wait till the hive is vacant before grabbing the honey—that had long been Antipas's motto. He thought it unwise to jail the man, but what could he do? Herodias had insisted. And generally, she was right about such things. The Baptist simply did not know how to keep his mouth shut.

Some people were just that way. Many of them members of his own family.

And now there was this other trouble maker too, one of his own subjects, from some trifling town near Sepphoris. Would the parade of would-be messiahs never end?

Antipas moved his cup slightly to the right, thereby reminding a sleepy steward of his duty.

"More wine, your Excellency?"

Antipas nodded, said nothing. Was it just him, he wondered? How could others not see that wine was very reminiscent of blood? Especially the thick, dark variety from Perea which they were now drinking. Yet it *tasted* fine. . . . Let poets dwell on the comparison.

At the table of Herod Antipas sat many of Galilee's notables—the wise and wealthy. All were there to ingratiate themselves with their monarch. The conversation had been light. There had been much laughter, promises of schemes to make everyone richer and happier. It was, after all, a good thing to eat with the king.

King is what Antipas rightly *should* have been. It had all been arranged. Herod the Great (as nowadays they were calling his deceased father) had clearly stipulated this in his will. Oh, Antipas knew very well he had not been his father's first choice. First in line to succeed were his sons by Mariamne: Alexander and Aristobulus. But they had proved too openly Roman and ambitious (a dangerous combination) and were promptly executed. Next, Herod the Great had pinned his hopes on Herod II. But only briefly, for his mother was implicated in an act of treason. Lastly, the old man turned to his first-born, Antipater. Another poor choice, for Antipater was the height of impatience; he tried to poison his father and hurry the process along. Herod executed him too.

Ah, thought Antipas, in sweet remembrance: finally it was *he* who was bumped to the front of the line.

Until, for some reason, on his deathbed, Herod *the so-called Great* changed his mind and made an entirely new will—trusting his legacy to none of his sons, and instead dividing his kingdom into three. Antipas was given only the second best portion.

To this day, Antipas ground his teeth at the memory of his father's spitefulness.

Their father's body was barely entombed before the two brothers were standing before authorities in Rome and disputing the terms of Herod's will. Antipas argued that the will was the product of a diseased mind, and therefore invalid. Archelaus insisted the will stand as written.

Archelaus won the day, but afterwards proved himself entirely incompetent, and if anything, even more impulsive and violent than his father. He kept his title but a few short years before being dismissed in disgrace. He exasperated the Roman authorities to such an extent that, from that point on, they decided to administer Judea themselves.

Great Father in Heaven! thought Antipas, banging his fist on his throne's armrest, if only they had given *him* Judea in the first place!

Antipas drained his cup and thrust the empty vessel back into the steward's hand. "Enough!" he said, directing his anger at the world in general, with particular reference to the ravages of time, intrigue, and Jewish politics.

"There, there," Herodias said to him, her soothing tones and soft hands, magic, as always, quickly restoring his equilibrium.

Always Herodias knew just what to say, what to do. Antipas smiled, then snickered, and began counting on his pudgy fingers: *First-born Antipater—gone, dead. The two curly-haired boys from Rome—gone, dead. Herod the Second, abandoned by Herodias—also gone, dead. Archelaus, disgraced, exiled—as good as dead.*

Only young Philip was left, Tetrarch of the North (a wasteland), no threat to anyone.

The only one remaining who mattered was Antipas himself. And with the help of his very able wife, the provinces might finally be reunited, giving Israel the king it had long pined for.

This was the plan. It was a very good plan.

Antipas turned admiring eyes toward his wife. How beautiful Herodias was, how intelligent, and how magnificently patient.

"Dearest," Herodias said, "I have a surprise for you."

"What is it, my love?"

"Since it is your birthday, something very special."

What could it be? A new jewel? A chest of silk from the East? Some new exotic creature from Nubia?

The drums began, and the flutes and cymbals joined in. A voluptuous young thing then whirled into the middle of the room with anklets jangling and hips as frisky as goats.

Antipas gasped. "Salome?" When Antipas had last seen Salome, she was a girl; now she was clearly something more.

"My daughter asked me specifically what gift she might offer to commemorate your birthday."

Antipas was bug-eyed, intoxicated by wine, dance, and drum. He squeezed his wife's arm. "This is a gift to surpass all others!"

Herodias smiled, said nothing.

"She is surely the image of you, Herodias, when you were this age!"

Again, a smile, no words.

Antipas called out: "Wonderful! Splendid!"

The dance bored into the tetrarch's brain. He clapped, he stamped his feet. Herodias's smile did not waver, even when Antipas wiped spittle from the side of his mouth. All the room swayed in rhythm to the dance and the beats of the drum. "More! More! Wonderful!" The shouts of Antipas's guests echoed his calls.

Salome finished with a flourish, arms thrown up in the air, and one knee touching the floor.

Antipas fixed his eyes on Salome's chest as it rose and fell rapidly like a little bird's. How could such a creature move so fast? With such a grace? And look! There were two beads of sweat swimming down the curve of her bare belly.

Antipas rose to his feet; Herodias steadied him. "Ask for anything, Salome, and it is yours!" Antipas looked over both shoulders at his guests, his wonderful guests, his friends; they cheered him on. "*Whatever you ask me, I will give you, even half of my kingdom.*"[75]

"It better be the Perean half!" one of his guests shouted.

When the laughter of the Galilean faction had subsided, Antipas staggered closer to his glistening step-daughter. "Anything, my daughter. Tell me what you wish."

Never had Antipas seen eyelashes so dark and long, highlighted by the deep violet of her eyelids. Salome glanced back at her mother whose smile had been locked in position since the start of the dance.

Antipas could not recall himself ever having been more sincere; he made his offer a third time, and placed his hand atop his step daughter's: "*Anything*, my sweet daughter."

Salome rose to her feet. Her scent was intoxicating. You could hear a pin drop in the great hall. "*I want you to give me at once the head of John the Baptist,*" she said finally. Her voice was neutral, emotionless. "*On a platter.*"[76]

It felt like a tree had crashed on Antipas's head. His smile collapsed, and he dropped Salome's hand. "This is truly what you want?"

One last time Salome glanced at her mother. "Yes," she replied.

For some moments, Antipas said nothing, *could* say nothing. Very gradually he began to nod his head, eyes turned away from Salome and fixed on the floor. He could see it all in a terrible flash: his dreams, his ambitions, all his patience and deserving . . . about to be decapitated.

The people would never forgive him.

After all the unpleasantness had passed, Antipas rose from his throne and accompanied Herodias out of the banquet room. For a moment, Antipas had been sad—quite sad. . . . But then an idea came to him—his very own idea, not one belonging to Herodias. After all, he told himself, people's memories were short and their allegiances fickle—this he had learned from his father. Herod had also taught him that ruling was mostly about distraction—bread and circuses—and if such a policy worked in Rome, why should it not work in Palestine? So . . .

Antipas rubbed his hands together and turned to Herodias. "My dear, I believe now would be the perfect time to go on a building spree. Do our civic duty!"

Who Touched Me?

Falling to her knees, Imma sobbed and gulped for air. She did this almost daily. Occasionally someone would stop, would be on the verge of asking how they could help. But then they would see who it was, saw that the woman in distress was unclean, and would do what any good Jew would do, and walk on.

What had Imma done to warrant such a curse? She had followed God's commands faithfully, cared for her husband without complaint, had always done everything people expected of her. Was it true then, what Scripture professed: that life was but a breath, a bent reed, and all was hopeless vanity?

It took all Imma's strength to lift her head—to acknowledge the carefree voices: merchants haggling, goats braying, small children giggling and swinging their clasped hands to and fro with their mothers. But where in this picture was there room for Imma? No happy smiles for her, no tiny flesh pressing against her palm.

The town square was noisier than usual. She didn't know why, nor did she care. Imma walked aimlessly, dragging her feet. The memory of three dead children lay heavy on her shoulders and stooped her back.

Praise the Lord for her husband, at least. He was, amidst all life's burdens, a consolation. He had not abandoned her, had not given up hope, had not spoken the dreaded words from Hosea: "She is not my wife, and I am not her husband," words meant to be spoken in anger before their children but . . . *what* children?

More than ten years sterile; it was enough; he might divorce her at any time.

If not to bear a child, what was her purpose? And if this was her purpose, why should God deny her? Not just deny her, but give the gift and almost immediately snatch it back? Three children she had cradled in her arms; sung over their tiny cries, watched their arms reach out and dark eyes search. For a breast, for love, for life itself.

Her last, a boy named Tobiah, shivered against her shoulder for the length of a dozen breaths—no more. He sighed, closed his tiny perfect eyes, then was gone—never to know the warmth of a rising sun.

Oh, Heavenly Father! Where is your justice? Where your compassion?

A ponderous gait and drooping eyes were marks of honor in a grandmother, but that is not how Imma had earned them. It was now twelve long years since Tobiah's death and, since then, no more false promises of children, no more heartbreaks and rending of clothes, only a dark muffled sorrow that clung to her limbs like soiled bandages she could not remove.

Why, oh Lord? Why this reminder? Following the phases of the moon, peaking at its fullness, the curse never abated completely—how could so much blood come from one person? It was no surprise her husband seldom touched her. No doctor, no amount of money, no priest, no prayers, no wise woman—nothing helped. This was her life: trudging, mourning and soaking up blood.

Sorrow was not Imma's lot alone. It followed the Lord's chosen like a cloud's dark shadow or a rogue wind, from a time and direction one could not influence. Even the town's elite, in their fine clothes, even the mothers blessed of many children, or the learned rabbis, even they, Imma figured, must hide in their hearts gaping wounds. All Imma might hope was that her wound—if not healed—might one day, at least bleed less.

"Rabbi!"

Could the owner of this panicky voice really be who she thought it was? Jairus? Keeper of the Meeting Place? Favored in Judea and respected by all? "Master!" he cried, "*My little daughter is at the point of death.*" The man was struggling for air. "She is my only daughter, Rabbi, twelve-years-old, her whole life before her!" Sobbing, Jairus fell at the Rabbi's feet. "*Come and lay your hands on her, so that she may be made well, and live.*"[77]

This must be the rabbi Imma had heard so much about, the one who healed the deaf, the blind, and lame. A good and holy man, a prophet surely. Unnoticed in the commotion, Imma was able to move closer.

The crowd was thick and buoyant (some, at least, anticipating another miracle.) They surrounded Jesus on all sides, jostling, getting as near as they could.

"This way!" Jairus called out.

"A good and holy man," Imma repeated to herself, having no thoughts beyond this, only praying on this one thought, that there *was* goodness in the world. She herself knew little of it, but it *must* exist. "Jesus," she said to herself, repeating the name, making a prayer of it. "Jesus," she whispered again, then sighed and folded her hands against her breast.

I might have had such a son.

The crowd began to tremble and move. Imma stretched out her fingers, wanting to touch, wanting tangible proof of the world's goodness, a moment's respite, a memento of virtue and hope.

The rabbi stopped suddenly. "*Who touched my clothes?*"[78] he asked.

The crowd quieted, considering this unlikely question. One of the Rabbi's disciples, squirming as he spoke, dared to answer: "Master, look at all these people pushing to and fro. *Many* people must have touched you."

Jesus stood on tiptoes, looking across the assembly. "Do you not understand, Peter? I felt the power going out of me." Then the Master locked eyes with Imma. The crowd parted before the two of them.

Jesus smiled and wrapped his hands around the woman's. "Do not fret."

"Forgive me, Rabbi! I only wished—"

"I know what you wished." Jesus gave a reassuring glance back at Jairus, then returned his attention to the woman. "*Daughter, your faith has made you well. Go in peace.*"[79]

Hardly had the crowd time to make sense of this episode, when a man came running into their midst. He beat his fist against his chest and cried, "Jairus, *your daughter is dead.* I am so sorry!" A second time, he beat his chest, then lowered his head and spoke softly: "My dearest friend, *why trouble the teacher any further?*"[80]

Jesus put a hand on Jairus's shoulder and whispered into his ear. Only Imma and those very near the grieving father could hear. "*Do not fear, only believe.*[81] *The child is not dead but sleeping.*"[82]

Jesus returned his attention to Imma. She beamed and spoke in a joyous, urgent whisper: "Go, Rabbi! She is only asleep, as you say, and I know you can wake her!"

Minutes later, Imma found the square deserted and peaceful. Quietly, with arms relaxed, and back straight, she sat on the ground, feeling as she had not felt in a very long time. She hummed to herself, a tune her mother had taught her when she was little. She savored that long ago memory, and the more recent memory too of what had just taken place between the Master and herself. *And*, Imma reminded herself—feeling her heart beating faster—the promise of what was *yet* to come!

A dove landed in front of her and cocked its head, aiming its pink eye at her, as if inquiring into her state of mind. Imma made no attempt to cover her mouth as she laughed out loud. "I am fine!" she cried out. "Very fine!" Because, Imma thought—rather, she *knew*—this day, *two* daughters had been blessed with new life.

The Stoning

The sun beats down, the winds blow, winter frost cracks our bones, and long buried, once again we turn our stony eyes upward.

What is the commotion above us? How to explain the restless shadows and the press of leather upon our heads? And the noise? Not grinding rock, not passing waves, not the sudden belching of subterranean fire—rather . . . an irritating titter . . . the sound of transient, weightless creatures, waking us from slumber.

"Teacher, this woman was caught in the very act of adultery."[83]

The tittering voices turn to grumbles, almost geologic, like storm clouds massing.

In bed with a man who was not her husband!

Shouts, great shuffling of feet, the one creature, distinct from the rest, stone-like, tumbles, spins, stumbles forward, comes to rest at the center. A woman—her head like granite, heavy and hanging—her clothes mere gossamer, snake skin ready to slough off. In and out she breathes, her short shadow heaving before the circle of stony men.

"Moses commanded us to stone such women."[84]

Then! Then! One of the men lays his warm fingers over me—a smooth wet warmth I have rarely known, only faintly remember. For once there were warm seas everywhere and also swimming creatures with sleek skin and great white teeth—giant shelled ammonites and clams, crinoids, all the world awash with shell and slippery water, and I and my fellows, happy particles suspended in this universe.

And there is more! All around me, my long buried fellows also are lifted up, cradled in sweaty palms, our rough contours fingered by eager flesh. How splendid is this! Again to be on the move! Skyward, breathing, eyes and ears open to a world working at light speed!

Cradled in disgruntled palms, we feel the ground beneath begin to tremble. The grumbles grow more coherent, rhythmic, a volcanic heart. Pressure builds. We move up and down to a throbbing chant:

Stone her! Stone the sinner! Stone her!

Like magma rising, the voices grow in strength. The man who holds me presses together his fingers, the most gentle of metamorphic squeezing, yet completely blocking out the light. No! I think. Is it my fate to be buried yet again? For who knows how long? With only this all too brief weightless memory?

What shall we do, Master?

And now I understand. I understand this sudden adoption, this pressing of stone to flesh and the awful destiny to which I'm called. Like a deep tectonic rumbling, the man's anger and fear pass from his blood and into my carbonate matrix. I am no longer to be myself. I am an extension of this creature. His explosiveness shall be *my* explosiveness. His wrath shall be *my* wrath. In a sudden eruption I am meant to hurl through air toward this bent-over woman standing in the center. Become unwilling stone of her flesh.

I am frozen, inanimate, desolate in my impotence.

Gradually the titters subside, like the tide ebbing or the magma settling. Still I feel the pressing upon me; I can feel it on the others too. All of us, we are enclosed in meaty and shaking fingers, waiting helplessly. Finally, there is a new, yet familiar, sound: a scratching in the sand, that age-old rhythm of stone scouring across seabed, snails and crabs skittering over endless grains of limestone. Dear, dear, sound—ancient writing below the waters.

What is he writing?
I can't see.
Why doesn't he answer us?
Master? the man holding me asks, *what are you writing?*

The Master remains silent; he continues moving his stick across the sand. Then! Oh joy! Fingers are unfurled, my body again greets the sun and I see all: a great circle of men stand on a hill, each with a stone in hand. Oh, Creator of All, I think, how is it I am blessed with sentience? How is it I hear all and see with godlike eyes? And why now?

The one writing in the sand now rises. With fierce sun-like eyes, he takes in everything: the sky, the ground, all stone and flesh together.

"Let anyone among you who is without sin be the first to throw a stone at her."[85]

The men shuffle their feet. Their breathing becomes fragmented, unrhythmic. The woman in the center looks at the man with the stick. He walks to her and offers a hand. Ah! I think. Contact metamorphism; it will change them forever!

One man cries out, *Bah!*

He flings his stone upon the ground beside his feet. I wince. It bounces twice, then comes to rest. Within that stone is a shark's tooth—my brother from an earlier time—a dream encased in a dream. The man leaves the circle.

Bah! cries another.

There are several exclamations, guttural, seismic. Stones slam upon the ground with increasing frequency. I wince again and again. Like shells pulled back by the tide, the men disperse, the hill grows bare till I too am released, for a moment, weightless.

Eons pass as I fall through the hard, clear air . Jerusalem! Dry as a bone! A city *today,* but under water not so very long before. . . . Now littered with noisy creatures who flood the land with their enduring restlessness.

I bounce three times and come to rest.

"Since no one condemns you, *neither do I condemn you*."

The woman kneels before the man and puts her lips to his feet. They whisper a few final words. The woman rises and leaves. Soon, all is still once more. As it has almost always been.

The sun beats down, the wind blows. Winter frosts await. Slowly the universe takes in a deep, deep breath.

Ah! I think, still falling. When will the universe finally exhale?

Transfigured

It was not the first time Peter had seen it, but still it puzzled him: how Jesus could walk down the steepest of paths and not stumble. Or was it simply that, by contrast, Peter was clumsy?

He did not *think* of himself as clumsy. In a fishing boat, no one was more agile, so why did he so frequently feel inadequate? Especially when it came to keeping up as they travelled from town to town. Or, in this case, walking down a mountain path.

"Why is the Rabbi always in such a hurry?"

"Maybe," John answered, "because there is so much to do."

Peter snorted. "As though fishermen do not know what it is like to be busy!"

James nodded in agreement. John said nothing.

Peter barrelled forward with his thoughts: "I tell you, my friends, if you walk that fast, eventually you're going to fall. And then where will you be?" Peter's heavy steps sent a stone bouncing downhill; it passed uncomfortably close to the Master.

Peter looked sheepishly at his two companions, determined nevertheless to keep on topic. "Slow and steady; that's my rule."

They continued downhill, restricting their conversation to whispers. In all likelihood, the Master was praying—silently, as he sometimes liked to do. Silent prayer had seemed strange at first, but now they were used to it—and they were careful not to interrupt.

John turned to his brother and to Peter: "You *do* understand what we saw up there?"

Peter answered with a gigantic shrug. "You tell *me*, John. Clearly *I* know nothing."

James came to Peter's defense: "Seeing is one thing, brother, but as for what it *means*. . . ."

"Exactly!"

"*Not so loud*, Peter." James put a hand over Peter's tense arm and spoke reassuringly: "Our time atop the mountain I will remember till the day I die—and Peter will too, I have no doubt—the sheer brilliance of it all. It was as if the Master were the sun itself, so bright, so pure. I had to shield my eyes."

"And his clothes, James! They were whiter than any laundry could ever make them!"

John raised a finger to his lips, reminding Peter.

"Yes, yes, I *know! Whisper!*" Peter rolled his eyes. "Keep going, James."

"What do you mean?"

"What did you see next?"

The question puzzled James. "We were all there together."

"Tell me anyway."

After a small sigh, James continued: "Next, two others appeared—I *know* you saw them, Peter—one on either side of the Master; they also shone like the sun."

John smiled and whispered: "More white than any laundry could make them."

Peter narrowed his eyes and lips, working extremely hard to control the loudness of his voice. "Then it wasn't just me! There *were* two others! Besides Jesus!"

"Yes," John assured Peter, "Moses and Elijah."

Peter repeated the names, shaking his head in wondrous recollection.

"And then . . ." James paused, as if considering whether to include further details. He turned to Peter. "You offered to make them shelters."

The memory stung him. "What was I *supposed* to do?"

Neither James nor John had an answer.

"Is it not the first law of hospitality? I was only . . ." Peter searched for the words; none would come. "In fact, I had *no idea* what I was doing!" For all Peter's missteps, the truth was his frequent companion.

The three men laughed—Peter too loudly. They collected themselves, and sheepishly walked on in silence, allowing the Master to pray without further distraction. Jesus did not look back.

James was first to dare speak again: "It was wonderful, most wonderful." James looked back up at the mountain. "But I confess, Peter—I was frightened too."

"*Thank* you!"

John then raised a finger, eager to make a point, it seemed. "Worst, and best of all, was when the shadow passed over."

"I'd forgotten about the shadow!"

John stared hard at Peter, as if to ask how anyone could forget such a thing? "And then," he continued, "we heard the Lord of Heaven's voice."

The three disciples spoke in unison: "*This is my Son, the Beloved.*"

John finished the quote: "*Listen to him.*"[86]

From here, they sank into a place beyond words. They looked at each other, amazed as much by their common memory as by the event itself.

The utter awe of the recollection helped Peter at last achieve a true whisper. "We saw *Moses. And* Elijah."

John added, "And our Heavenly Father's Son."

Another period of silence followed. Then from Peter's furrowed brow, a new thought found its final form, and prophetic words fell from his lips: "Remember Moses? Back in Sinai? When he came down from the mountain?"

John turned his head sharply, attentive. "With the Holy Tablets. Yes, Peter."

"And how his face—how did the Holy Book put it, John? How it . . . *glowed.*"

"He had been speaking with 'I Am Who I Am'; he was a man transformed."

Peter shrugged and kept his eyes fixed on the ground: "That's all I'm saying."

The recollection of their time atop the mountain preoccupied them and nourished them till finally the path levelled out. Jesus came to a stop. He turned around and addressed his disciples: "Share this with no one."

The disciples nodded. It was no great burden; who would believe them?

"Until," Jesus concluded, "the Son of Man has risen from the dead."

Then the Master turned his gaze toward their destination, six or seven hundred cubits down the road.

So, thought Peter, they might make it back before sunset after all, and the fox might find his den.

Jesus paused only long enough for a quick drink from his water skin; then he was off, leaving his disciples needing to race to catch up. Peter stumbled, then recovered. He gulped for air and grabbed John by the shoulder: "What did the Master mean, do you think? 'Risen from the dead'?"

Full Circle

"Go to Jerusalem," his friends liked to say. It was friendly advice, meant to be helpful.

Daniel was the worst, putting a hand on Lazarus's shoulder and smiling like an idiot: "And when they hear it is *you* looking for work—well, there is no question—who would not want a cabinet built by the famous Lazarus of Bethany?"

Lazarus wanted to scream.

"Come, come," Daniel kept insisting. "I'm going to Jerusalem tomorrow. We can go together."

Yes, a cabinet made by Lazarus of Bethany, the man Jesus raised from the dead—a great novelty. No doubt, it would fetch a good price. Lazarus bristled at the thought, and returned to his work. There was always the work, if nothing else. No one to *buy* the work necessarily, but there was the work itself: taking a piece of wood, shaping it, fastening one piece to another, participating in the Lord's great act of creation. It was enough; it *had* to be enough.

Martha stepped into the workshop. "I thought I should tell you; our Lord is coming."

Lazarus pretended not to understand.

"*Jesus*," Martha said. She paused, trying to make her brother look her in the eye. "You know very well who I mean." Martha quickly scanned the workshop, peering over her brother's shoulder and past a jumble of tools and piled wood. "Have you seen Mary?"

Lazarus shrugged his massive shoulders. They had been big *before* he died; now they were bigger.

Martha swallowed a sigh. "Then I suppose it will be left to just me to prepare the food again."

The gleam in Martha's eye did not match the tone of her voice; this confused Lazarus. Many things confused him lately.

Martha shook her head and clucked her tongue. "Oh Mary, Mary, Mary. . . . It is not only *you* who loves the Lord, nor should it be only *me* who does the cooking!"

It's not as if Lazarus didn't *want* to meet the Master again. But what would he say? What would they talk about? *How does it feel to be risen from the dead?* Was there any question Lazarus dreaded more? He just didn't want to talk about it. Why did people not understand this? In the first few months, people would come to him regularly, complete strangers, all asking variations of that same question, till Lazarus felt his head ready to explode. He had nothing to say. Not even to the priests and Pharisees, *especially* to the Pharisees.

Is it true that Jesus of Nazareth raised you from the dead?

Yes, Lazarus would reply. And that was it. Case closed.

Finally, the curious grew bored and stopped coming. Until the other day, when two new Pharisees arrived; Lazarus could see them from his workshop. They were standing on a nearby hill and pointing in his direction. But they did not come in or call to him. They just looked, nodding their heads. Lazarus was uneasy for the rest of the day.

Jesus arrived mid-afternoon along with several of his disciples. The usual crowd followed behind: the curious, the beggars, the sick—all looking for another miracle—though it would not involve Lazarus *this* time. Many were singing and laughing.

Lazarus watched his sister re-enter the house and thanked the Lord he had not been born a woman. He was not without sympathy; Martha must be going crazy, thinking of the horde that would soon swamp her doorstep, all expecting something to drink, bread, olives—who knew what else? It was too much for one woman, for *two* women.

At the very end of the parade, Lazarus spied some temple priests and the same two Pharisees he had noticed the day before. More than anything, it was their lack of laughter and singing that set them apart.

Fortunately, Martha's hospitality needed to extend only to the dozen or so guests now seated at her table. Outside, the hangers-on and Pharisees seemed content simply to sit and eavesdrop on the conversations from inside. Sighing, Lazarus seated himself at the place nearest the door. Jesus sat opposite him.

As Martha passed by with a basket of fruit, Jesus touched her arm and whispered to her. The words made her smile. After setting down the food, Martha returned to the kitchen, her step light, and her face glowing, enjoying a minor kind of resurrection, Lazarus mused. He quickly flung the blasphemous thought aside.

Jesus had just begun to break the bread and was passing it down the table. Finally, in walked Mary.[87] She looked disheveled, as though she'd been running. "I'm so sorry!" she cried.

Jesus answered, "Greetings, Mary! We are so blessed you are here."

Mary was carrying a large, decorative jar, and already the scent from its contents was wafting through the room. She reached for a nearby basin and lifted the Master's feet and set them gently into the basin. She threw her shawl back over her shoulder and knelt beside Jesus. She poured from her jar till the scented oil splashed luxuriously over the Master's feet. Her tears joined the mixture.

Everyone looked; no one spoke. Mary unfastened her hair and used it to dry Jesus's feet. Martha watched from the kitchen. She too said nothing, but there was no scowl on her face, no hint of irritation, rather a—Lazarus couldn't find the word. An acceptance? A resignation? Lazarus grunted and looked at his own feet. He had never truly understood his sisters.

Lazarus, and every single Jew, knew what the custom was. You honor your guests—especially guests who had travelled far—by washing their feet. This should have been Lazarus's job. At least to provide the water! How could he forget? He felt stupid, ashamed. But it was always this way when he was around the Rabbi. It was all he could do to remember his own name. And yet, beyond the embarrassment and confusion, Lazarus could sense a feeling of *peace* settling on the room. It clung to every corner, to the rafters, to the tabletop, to their very tunics. Lazarus had known nothing of peace since the day he had stumbled out of the tomb.

They finished the meal. Jesus gave a final blessing. He rose and walked over to Lazarus and put a hand on his shoulder. "Peace be with you, my brother."

Lazarus replied weakly, "And with you, Master."

Then Jesus went to speak to the people camped outside. Mary, as well as Martha, followed. Good for Martha, thought Lazarus.

Once Jesus was out of hearing range, one of his disciples banged a fist on the table and growled: "Am I the only one who is outraged?"

"Outraged?" Simon Peter asked.

"Why was this perfume not sold for three hundred denarii and the money given to the poor?"[88]

It was a question which had occurred to Lazarus himself, and judging by the pained look on the faces of some of the other apostles, many shared his uneasiness.

Judas was just getting started. "I would gladly have washed the Master's feet myself, and saved a year's wages!"

"The perfume cost that much?" asked the disciple called Thomas.

Judas leaned his head low across the table as if ready to share a conspiracy. "Think what the poor could have done with this money!"

They were all startled to find Jesus standing at the door's threshold. The setting sun cast him in silhouette and outlined his body in a golden light.

"Dear Judas," Jesus said, *"you always have the poor with you."* Everyone stared at Judas, then back at Jesus. *"But you do not always have me."*[89]

Simon Peter squirmed in his chair. John put a hand over his arm, as if to restrain him. Mary and Martha re-entered the house a moment later, sheepishly squeezing past the Master, first kissing his hand, and then retreating together to the kitchen.

Jesus spoke again: "Do not judge our sister Mary. This perfume is for the day of my burial."

The apostles all looked at one another; here was another of Jesus's sayings which defied understanding.

The next morning, before departing, Jesus stopped to speak to Lazarus in his shop. "My friend," he said, "work will pick up, I promise." He patted Lazarus on the shoulder. "A Roman official will request some crosses. Do not refuse the work."

Never Ridden

His ears twitched and his tail curled up, rhythmically swatting at flies. So it had always been and would always be, like a great heartbeat that defined the rhythm of his days. Most insistent of all was the never-ending hiss of human voices, calling from every direction, yelling, imploring—who knew what they were about?

Adam had begun to notice a secondary rhythm also: longer days, the sun rising higher, and the stick on his back more frequent; all these signs seemed connected to a great increase in human activity. Even his own master—fair-minded, for the most part—fell prey to this rising frenzy. His voice rose in pitch. His steps grew more frantic. There were frequent, heated exchanges with his mate—he *thought* it was the master's mate—it was not so easy to tell. Sometimes their exchanges were more like donkey groans than words. Very puzzling indeed. Adam chewed and blinked his eyes; the ways of humans, he reckoned, were beyond a donkey's ken.

Breaking through the midday din, a different sort of babble caught Adam's attention. It was more ordered and repetitive, like birds. For several days now, this had been the pattern. Adam remembered how this bird-speak had annoyed him initially. Now it was not so bad; he knew what to expect. Quite possibly, it mellowed his master's heart, which could only be a good thing.

As the morning progressed, a long parade of donkeys climbed the road leading out of the valley and into the village. Some carried people on their backs. To Adam, the sight seemed incredible. It was one thing to carry bags of vegetables, or firewood, or furniture, but to have the legs of an actual person straddle your back? One who, at any moment, might beat you or else (and maybe this made the risk all worthwhile) rub your forehead and whisper into your ear? This would be a different experience entirely.

Steadily, the donkeys plodded past him. By their smells alone, Adam could tell their age, their readiness for mating, every important detail about them. An exchange of glances would be superfluous and would only earn them a stick and a harsh word, so the passing donkeys restricted their focus to the backside directly in front of them.

It struck Adam as strange that he was not among the parade. Hardly a day went by when he was not called upon—carrying this and that—but today, for some reason, he remained tethered near the door.

Had he done something to offend his master?

Two men came running, breaking away from the busy convoy of men and beasts. They came straight toward Adam, stopping only at the last moment. Adam huffed softly, studied them with his left eye. He could not help shivering.

"This must be the one the Master meant!" The man's eyes were open very wide, as if he were frightened, or possibly surprised, or maybe both. Reading human faces was not Adam's strong suit.

" 'As you enter the village' he said, right?" The other man also had large eyes. It was difficult to tell the two men apart. "Well, we've entered the village, and there's the donkey tethered outside the door, just as the Master said."

Growing more nervous, Adam began to shuffle his hooves. What were these strange men doing and what were they saying? It would be so much easier if he could just read their smells, but human smells were utterly chaotic. Whatever information they contained was jumbled, often meaningless.

"We can't just *take* it," said the first man, "can we?"

"Relax, Thomas, it's what the Master told us to do."

Master—it was one of the few words Adam was certain of. What could these strangers mean? Neither of them was his master.

The one called Thomas said, "Andrew, I'm not so sure about this."

"*I'll* do it then."

Thomas stayed back, while the one called Andrew moved closer. He patted Adam on the forehead. "Easy, my friend." His words were soft and soothing. Then he searched for the knot in the tether and began to unravel it. "Today is your lucky day. You get to meet the Master."

Again that word. What did his master have to do with any of this? It was very confusing.

Still standing back, Thomas looked over his shoulder. "Hurry!" he shouted. Several men had stepped out from the procession and were pointing in Thomas's direction.

Just then, the blue-painted door swung open, and out stepped Adam's true master. He raised his hand to shield the sun from his eyes. His voice was gruff. Adam braced himself, half-expecting a beating. "You there," he asked. "What are you doing?"

One of the onlookers, pointed and said, "Someone is stealing your donkey." In his other hand, the man held a good-sized stone.

Adam could feel the tremor in Andrew's arms pass all the way down through his tether.

"Please, sir," Andrew said, "our rabbi told us we would find a young donkey tethered near a door. We only mean to borrow the animal."

Thomas rushed up to join his partner. He was out of breath, which surprised Adam, for the distance the stranger had run had not been very great. "A donkey that has never before been ridden."

Adam's master glared back at the strangers. "My donkey never *has* been ridden. What of it?"

Grinning, Andrew exclaimed, "Then we are in the right place!"

The crowd had now grown to a dozen men and was slowly closing in. "Sir!" Thomas added quickly, "our rabbi needs your donkey—though we're not sure why." The crowd was only ten paces away. "But we promise to bring it back just as soon as we can!"

Adam's master stepped forward. He was within easy reach of both the tether and Andrew's throat. "Who is this rabbi you speak of?"

"Jesus of Nazareth."

"Of *Nazareth*?"

Thomas turned and pointed behind him. "A little town in Galilee. Just east of—"

"I *know* where Nazareth is." Adam's master paused—it was the pauses which Adam feared most, but a timely pat on the back reassured him. His master circled to the other side and patted him a second time, on the forehead and then the cheek. Adam could not help but whinny and close his eyes. *Please, master, pat me like this forever. . . .*

Adam's master kept his eyes fixed on the two would-be thieves. Firmly, but not violently, he removed the tether from Andrew's grip. "He's called Adam."

"What?"

"My donkey." The master's smile was hard to see, but Adam knew it was there. "Because he is first-born."

"Oh!"

Again, a silence fell between the men, including among the bystanders. This was the moment of truth. Adam's master extended his hand and passed the tether back to Andrew. "Go ahead then." Adam felt a firm and steady pat on his back. It made him blink and snort. "Take him," the master said. "With my compliments to the rabbi."

It was like beams of light from a sun shower, the way relief broke over the two strangers' faces. The one called Thomas did a little dance. "Yes! Yes! Thank you! We will! We'll bring him back very soon, we promise!"

The bystanders parted, making way for the two men and the donkey. The man holding the stone let it drop.

Led by his bridle, Adam clopped downhill at a good pace, against the flow of pilgrims. The avalanche of smells rushed gleefully into his nostrils: so many sweet and sour aromas, so many donkeys—many of whom he recognized. Even a few horses, goats and sheep, birds in cages, and all manner of noisy humans with their bird-speak rising and rolling like the hills they trod upon. It was enthralling. And the two men leading him—not once did they hit Adam with a rod. They were too busy laughing and bird-speaking; it was all very new and exciting.

Finally, they seemed to reach their destination. Someone brought Adam a bowl of water, and he drank deeply. Many hands stroked his head. The people laughed more than they spoke.

"Rabbi," one from the crowd said, "here is your royal mount! Andrew tells us his name is Adam."

"Ah," a voice answered, the words very sweet and reassuring, "the new Adam."

A moment later, Adam felt fabric being loaded on his back, but nothing rough: soft linens, blankets, one after another, light and warm—what on earth was going on? Finally, a great happy shout arose. From his left eye, Adam saw the shadows of two men, then a third man whose dark shape climbed somewhere above him. Then the man must have slid downwards, settling on his back! On his *back*, yes! And gentle voices were whispering and men's hands were stroking him—very, very gently with a palm frond.

"Forward, my friend! Into the city!"

Adam understood little of what was happening, but he knew that it was good. "Forward!" came the cry once more. This was a word Adam knew, and he obeyed. He brayed. The crowd laughed, and once again, bird-speak was in the air:

> Blessed is the king who comes in the name of the Lord!
> Peace in heaven, and glory in the highest heaven![90]

Before Adam lay a road covered with tunics and palm fronds. And the bird-speak went on, and the laughing, and the dancing, and the feel of the man upon his back—such a feeling! It felt as if the man belonged there. As if the two of them were actually one. Indeed, as if all that surrounded him were one, and there were no boundaries between beast and tree and sky.

How wonderful! thought Adam. The idea of wonderful had never before entered his mind. He hardly knew what it meant, except that it was true! It was wonderful! To have this man upon his back, the Master, the Rabbi, his Lord!

All too soon the journey ended—a thousand steps, ten thousand—who knew? The man descended from his back. The blankets and clothes were removed and the two strangers took Adam back to his village and tether.

"Thank you, good friend," they said to him. "You served the Master well!"

Adam watched the men disappear up the road. He looked into the setting sun and reflected as much as was in his power. What did he feel exactly?

It was not relief. Not the relief that might reasonably be expected when a burden was lifted from your back. Rather, it was as if . . . it was as if the world were *more* than donkeys and men, more than food and drink and sleep. It was as if the world were much bigger than Adam had ever imagined, and through some great stroke of fortune, this day he had participated in that bigness.

Adam glanced up at the setting sun and shook his limbs and brayed more loudly than he had ever done. It did not much matter than he only faintly understood why.

Not the One

Naomi had told him he was "too holy" and therefore she would not marry him. "Only our Father in Heaven is holy," Barak had replied. "Pure then," Naomi said, "You are *too pure*." Barak drew two conclusions from Naomi's judgement: one, his Heavenly Father never meant him to marry. And two, there was no reason he should not now strive to be *more* pure.

It was Barak's favorite time of day: the hour before the world awoke. He watched the sky grow golden in the eastern hills and would not mind if this hour stretched out to eternity.

He walked slowly from his quarters, relishing the sound of his papyrus sandals slapping against the polished stones of the empty courtyard. It would be some time yet before the pilgrims stood outside the gate, and this was as it should be.

Barak was blessed among the blessed: a high priest, a descendant of Zadok, unblemished, an esteemed member of the Sanhedrin, and a learned scribe as well. Who else could say as much? It was only fitting that he stand at the threshold of the Priest's Court, within sight of the holiest of holies.

It was true that Jerusalem's holy temple was incomplete, but what *was* finished was magnificent—even to the eyes of Gentiles! What was still to come could be vividly imagined with a careful reading from the Book of Ezekiel.

All this magnificence they owed to the work of the puppet-king Herod—cursed be his name. And yet Barak had to admit, the Lord could work in ways beyond men's understanding. If it was through pagan hands that his temple must be rebuilt, so it must be, for the Lord on High (blessed be his name) could never be wrong! Barak put a hand to his bearded chin. It could be, he thought, that Herod was not Rome's puppet after all, but the Lord's!

For all the blessings Barak enjoyed, it would be a mistake of the gravest kind to rest upon his laurels. The enemies of Israel were everywhere; sometimes obvious and large like the occupying Roman army but, more often than not, subtle as dust in a kitchen corner, or a bird's whisper in a cave. An attitude of vigilance was the first requirement for every temple priest.

There was a time—not so long ago—when the Chief Priest's word was law. It held absolute authority over every Hebrew heart. There was complete unity throughout the land of Israel, but now—Barak could only shake his head and pull his beard—the days of David and Solomon—how far away those times seemed! Their current chief priest, Caiaphas, was neither David nor Solomon. And, being neither, he was "tolerated" by the Romans.

Barak despised the word. Where would the Hebrew people be if toleration were their ideal? Their Heavenly Father demanded love and obedience, not toleration!

Barak curled his lips into a smile. Had not his people defeated the Seleucids? This was no act of toleration. All the known world had crumbled before one pagan empire after another, but not Barak's people, not the Macabees. *They* had the law of Moses. And the law had *them*.

Call them stubborn, wilful, incapable of compromise, backward— Barak had heard it all and worse, but the truth was inescapable—the people of Israel would never yield. *Could* not yield. The salvation of the world depended on their steadfastness.

Barak turned at the sound of leather sandals scuffing over the marble stairway to his left. "Greetings and blessings!" a voice cried. It was one of the Levites. Barak did not know his name. He was preparing to receive the multitude of animals that would be brought for sacrifice this day. "Blessings upon you," Barak replied, grudgingly acknowledging the dedication this Levite showed for his duties. Barak had made it a point of honor to be first up among the clergy, and had no wish to be usurped by an underling.

And really, what was one to make of these Levites? So earnest in their duties, but so inscrutable in their thoughts. Barak had never exchanged more than a few pleasantries with them; he had little idea what they thought about anything, if they thought at all. Temple business could not proceed without them—this much he conceded. But how strange it was that the tribe of Levi—chosen by Moses himself to be the priestly caste—should come to this, to be mere servants, not priests at all. What great past sin had reduced them so?

Daily Barak gave thanks to the heavenly angels that he had not been born to the tribe of Levi.

The east had brightened considerably; wisps of pink clouds now highlighted the saffron sky. From below, and outside the temple walls, Barak could faintly hear the the cooing of caged birds and the lowing of doomed cattle. With Passover so near, the troughs would run thick with blood this day, and the smell of burnt flesh would fill the city air. Not that Barak himself would smell it. Long ago he had lost his sense of smell—a curse, he had thought, at first. But now he understood the affliction for what it was, yet another of his Eternal Father's blessings.

The first glint of sun—it was time! Barak smiled to hear the groan of metal and muscle as twenty men pushed open the great bronze doors of the Nicanor Gate. Barak gave the signal. A blast of trumpets filled the air and spread like heavenly messengers across Jerusalem's rooftops. The voices of pilgrims rose in a joyous shout and began to chant in unison with their high priest: *Shema Israel!*

Their morning prayer done, Barak gazed out at the faithful who stood below. They were so varied: some poor, some rich, some from the far reaches of the Mediterranean, yet all of them, Israel's chosen. Among them, of course, were his fellow priests, most of whom, to Barak's considerable chagrin, were Sadducees.

It riled Barak repeatedly, how the Sadducees spoke so often of not wanting to offend the Romans. Really? *They?* Offend the *Romans?* Was it not Pilate who chose to enter the holy city with his imperial standard? Or Herod, Rome's puppet, trying to do much the same outside the Temple's holy sanctuary? The list of sacrileges was long.

But, they would argue, consider how the Romans respect our customs. We do not have to serve in their army. We are still allowed to collect our Temple tax and celebrate all our feasts. They waive for us the requirement to worship their emperor.

Because we would rather die first! Because if they allowed us in their armies, we would rebel! All these "concessions" as you call them, Rome allows to us only *because* we resist!

And on and on the argument would go, and Barak would end up rolling his eyes, muttering to himself, and despairing for his people's future.

The Court of the Gentiles must be packed. The din alone was enough to assure Barak of this. The moneychangers would be busy at their stalls, and cattle cries of every variety would be mixing with the heavily accented voices of the Diaspora. Barak had witnessed the hysteria many times; he had no need to see it this day. The crowd moved in a predictable rhythm: first through the Court of the Gentiles, then through the Beautiful Gate and into the Temple Proper (first leaving the women behind), and finally up another fifteen steps and into the Court of the Israelites. There the men would linger, praying, hands raised to heaven and eyes cast to the ground.

One man ignored the routine, seeming to care for neither prayer nor sacrifice. He moved remarkably fast for a man with a limp, and headed straight for the high priest who momentarily feared for his life.

The terror passed quickly, as did the embarrassment.

"My Lord!" the man cried. He was panting and sweating as he knelt at the priest's feet. "I need to speak with you."

It was hard to see what business this peasant could have with a high priest. "What do you need to speak about?" Barak asked.

"Jesus of Nazareth—I know the man."

This day might hold some interest after all.

"I am one of his followers." The man would not look up from the ground. He struggled to find his words. "I could take you to him."

The Holy One was abundant in his blessings. Everything happened for a reason. Sometimes Barak doubted this teaching, but here it was reinforced with authority. "Stay here," Barak said.

Barak returned with two fellow priests, and they made this unlikely informant follow them to a small alcove which was quieter and out of the way. The priests sat on soft cushions behind a table while the disciple remained standing, pulling nervously on the tassels of his sleeves.

Barak began the interrogation: "You were telling me you know this rabbi of Nazareth personally, and his whereabouts."

"Yes."

"And *your* name?"

"Judas."

"But not from Galilee, judging by your accent?"

Head hung low, Judas pointed behind him. "From Kerioth."

This detail was of no importance. The priest to Barak's left asked: "Why exactly are you here, Judas?'

The informant shifted his weight from foot to foot, and shook his head. It was as if he had not thought through any of this—had not anticipated questions at all. Finally, he managed to stammer: "I thought you might be interested."

"In what exactly?"

"Interested in . . . talking to him—*stopping* him."

The priest to Barak's right asked, "Stopping him from what?"

"I don't know!" Judas cried out. "I only know he is not the one!"

Both Barak's colleagues were Sadducees, but sure to be of one mind when it came to false prophets. Barak whispered to them: "I have it on good authority that our Galilean madman said he would tear down the Temple in three days and then raise it again! Can you imagine?"

"I cannot!"

The priest on the left leaned toward Barak and whispered back: "Has this blasphemer many followers?"

Barak was as knowledgeable about the city's rumors as anyone. "Not many as yet, but they say he is charismatic, and his numbers grow. What can I say?" Barak raised his hands into the air and smiled sardonically. "Galilee seems to breed madmen like flies."

And, Barak thought to himself, always better to stamp out a fire when it is yet small.

The priest on the right spoke again: "Clearly, young man, you are a pious Hebrew who is only doing his religious duty."

Judas said nothing.

"Can you lead us to your rabbi?"

The other said, "We would be most eager to speak with him."

Judas nodded.

Barak's heart leapt with anticipation. At last! A chance to make a difference! He forced himself to speak slowly and contain his excitement: "Where and when?"

Judas seemed on the verge of bolting, so Barak added quickly, "Of course, we intend to pay you for your trouble." Barak reached into his robe and found his money bag. He counted out ten denarii and stacked them neatly on the table. "Such information is invaluable, Judas, as you anticipated. Certainly worth ten pieces of silver. . . ." The high priest had hooked his fish; he needed only to net it. "Let's make it twenty." A second neat stack was pushed up beside the first. "A man such as yourself clearly has expenses to consider."

Judas's arms were shaking and his eyes darted back and forth.

Barak was *so* close. He must be careful not to spook his prey. He glared at his fellow priests who finally understood, and slowly reached into their own money bags, each adding another five coins to the bribe.

The important thing, Barak reminded himself, was to display confidence and calm—as a priest should always strive to do. Barak thought himself quite good at this. After just the right amount of waiting, he scooped the coins up from the table and walked slowly toward Judas. It was like approaching a skittish kitten—one false step. . . . "There, my friend." Barak held up two palms full of glinting silver. "All for you. Now, where did you say we could find your master?"

Judas cleared this throat, then spoke: "In the garden of Gethsemane. Tonight. We often go there to pray." Judas looked at the other two priests. Whatever reassurance he hoped to find on their faces was not there.

"And how will we know him?"

"He'll be the first one I greet." Judas shrugged and shook his head. "There is nothing else I can tell you."

It was enough; Barak smiled. "Thank you, Judas of Kerioth. Tonight then."

Judas turned to leave.

"My good and true Hebrew, aren't you forgetting something?"

It took an inexplicably long time for Judas to realize what he was to do. Finally, he stepped forward and put his cupped palms under the priest's. Barak let the coins slide through. The sound of their clanging together seemed to startle Judas. One of the coins missed its mark, and began to bounce and roll down the polished steps, heading toward the Nicanor Gate.

Smiling, and in his most fatherly tone, Barak whispered to his informant: "Well, *I'm* not going to fetch it."

Feed Them

Jerusalem was nothing like Bethsaida. Its streets were noisy and bright and smelly and—what could you call the place but . . . *alive!* Best of all, there were rumors that the Master was also here.

"Watch where you're going, boy!"

Constantly men with long beards jostled Jonathan and pushed him aside. They had clear destinations and pressing engagements, whereas Jonathan—he was like a leaf in the wind. He laughed at the thought, doing a half-twirl, as yet another Levite bumped against his shoulder.

"Apologies!" Jonathan cried out, the smile on his face trumping any sense of embarrassment they might expect him to feel. And that they should call him "boy"—what did that matter? *He* knew how old he was. He was fourteen, a shepherd's son, sturdy, reliable and, by himself, had walked all the way to Jerusalem. How many of these Levites could have done *that*?

Jonathan asked directions from a dozen different strangers, till finally he found his way to his cousin's house. Eli and Sapphira welcomed him as if he were their own son. They fed him, they washed his feet, and offered him their best chair. In the evening, Eli suggested they go to the local synagogue. "Jonathan," his cousin said to him, poking him in the chest with a finger, "don't forget to bring your basket."

It was the second greatest day of Jonathan's life.

Eli's face beamed as he introduced his young cousin. "This is Jonathan, son of Noah of Bethsaida. He has seen the Master *in person*, and *spoken* with him."

"Indeed," a number of elders mumbled, stroking their beards. One named Ananias said, "We would be very interested in knowing what the Master said to you."

Never before had Jonathan attracted such attention; never had complete strangers seemed to hang on his every word. He answered with a smile and stammer, "Not much."

Ananias leaned closer and winked. "He must have said *something*."

"I remember he asked to look at my basket." Jonathan held up the object in question. "This one here."

Jonathan's cousin took up the slack. "You've heard about Jesus feeding the five thousand?" He put a hand around his cousin's shoulder and squeezed. "Jonathan was *there*—Bethsaida is his home town. He saw the whole thing!"

The murmur among the elders grew into a small roar until Ananias, the de facto leader of the assembly, raised a hand and called for order. He moved very close to young Jonathan. "Tell us what happened, my son." He put his large, weathered hand over the boy's. "Take your time."

Taking a deep breath, Jonathan looked out over his audience who sat in a large semi-circle. "Someone said they had seen the Master walking toward the hills."

"Coming from where?" another elder asked.

Jonathan shrugged. "From across the lake? I'm not sure."

Another murmur rose from the crowd. This surprised Jonathan because, so far, nothing in his tale was out of the ordinary.

"And then?" Ananias asked.

"Then everyone pretty much dropped what they were doing. I had fallen asleep, so my uncle shook my shoulder." This detail elicited a few laughs from his listeners and encouraged Jonathan in a way he didn't quite understand.

" 'Jonathan!' my uncle said to me, 'you can sleep later. Come, we don't want to miss this!' So then I did as I was told, and followed." Jonathan paused. It was good to have an audience in the palm of his hand. "Though, in truth, I wished I could have slept longer."

The elders laughed.

Jonathan enjoyed the laughter, but it suddenly struck him that his listeners might get the wrong idea. "That's what I thought *at first. Later*, of course, I was very glad I went. *Very, very* glad."

"So," Ananias said, steering Jonathan's story back on course, "half the town followed Jesus into the hills."

"More than half, sir."

"Even the lame, the blind?"

"Especially them."

Ananias scanned the assembly, making sure they were all attentive. "And the Nazarene healed them all?"

"I don't know about *all*, Rabbi, but the ones I saw, yes."

There were more murmurs, even grumbles. Not everyone seemed pleased by Jonathan's account.

Again Ananias raised a hand. It took some time, but finally the voices stilled. "Tell us of the Nazarene's teachings."

Jonathan shook his head. "I only know that he told wonderful stories."

"How were they wonderful?"

Jonathan smiled at the memory. "It's hard to say, Rabbi. Some stories were funny, many surprising, some made me question things I had never thought about before. You should go to hear him yourself, sir."

Ananias smiled. "So I should."

Eli decided his cousin needed a nudge. "Tell them the best part," he whispered. Momentarily Jonathan was puzzled. How could there be a *best part*?

"About the loaves and fishes."

It seemed as if Ananias could read minds for, a moment later, he said: "Young man, tell us why Jesus wanted to see your basket?"

Jonathan stared at the golden sky in the west. The last rays of the sun glinted off the balustrade on the Temple roof. He could hear distant voices reciting a prayer. It was beautiful beyond words. How burdensome to have to rely on words! But what choice did he have? "It was about this same time of day, sir—just after sunset. Looking around, I could see that no one seemed to have brought anything to eat."

"Except you?"

Again the elders laughed. At him or with him? Jonathan was no longer sure. Eli patted his cousin on the shoulder.

"I had five loaves and two fish which I promised to bring to my aunt, but in the confusion, I just ran with the others into the hills, clutching my basket all the way, almost forgetting I had it in my hand."

"Ah," said Ananias, nodding and turning to his peers, "the enthusiasm of youth!" Then back to Jonathan, "What did Jesus do then?"

"He asked to borrow my basket. I figured he must have been hungry after all that talking."

Ananias pointed to the basket. Jonathan nodded, confirming to all that this was the very basket.

"Of course I told the Master yes. Then he took one of the loaves and raised it into the air and whispered something—a blessing, I suppose. He did the same with the fish."

Jonathan paused, waiting for a response from the elders, but there was only silence; they were all looking at him, waiting. For what, Jonathan did not know. He was no storyteller. Finally, Ananias spoke: "Continue, my son."

"I didn't catch all of it, but the Master definitely said something about feeding the people."

"Meaning all the people gathered on the hill, the many thousands?"

"That's what I took him to mean, Rabbi, yes."

"Extraordinary."

"To be honest, sir, some of his disciples didn't seem too happy. One, I think his name was Philip, rolled his eyes—I remember that." Jonathan demonstrated with a roll of his own, making the elders laugh yet again.

Ananias resumed his questioning: "And Jesus's followers were unhappy because . . ."

"Well, if they were like me, Rabbi, they were wondering how five loaves and two fish could feed all those people."

Now the murmurs turned into an uproar; there seemed to be factions, a debate between two groups considering the meaning of Jonathan's words. Only Ananias's stern hand once more brought order to the proceedings.

Ananias raised his massive eyebrows to their maximum height. "And so you fed them? All of them?"

"I just carried the basket, Rabbi. It was the disciples who passed out the food. Jesus had arranged everyone into blocks—I don't know, maybe fifty people to a block—and we walked from group to group. I'd hand out a loaf and a fish, and two of the disciples would pass them down the rows."

Ananias put hands on both Jonathan's shoulders, looking him in the eye. "But surely, son, after you passed out the fifth loaf and the second fish, you would have had an empty basket."

Jonathan smiled. "No, sir."

Again the elders erupted. This time Ananias ignored them. "You *saw* this? With your own eyes?"

"I ate some of the bread myself. It was good bread. And you'd think, after being out in the sun most the day, the fish wouldn't be so good, but it was good too." Jonathan laughed at the memory. He remembered how, on the day, he had also laughed—laughed and laughed. The two apostles kept patting him on the shoulder, as if it were *Jonathan* who was performing this magic trick, not Jesus—but everyone knew better. "I kept looking into the basket, Rabbi, again and again, wondering if this time that would be the last loaf, but after a while, I stopped looking."

Jonathan studied his audience; most of the men were smiling. Some of their faces were even ... *radiant*. But a few were scowling. Some elders even rose to their feet, ready to walk away, until Ananias stopped them.

"So, my friends," he said, "thanks to young Jonathan here, we have a firsthand account of one of the Nazarene's many miracles. If this boy's story is to be believed, a miracle is indeed what took place. Perhaps the stories are true, and the Messiah is in our midst."

One of the elders spat on the ground. "How can anything good come from Galilee?"

"Do we know the mind of God?" Ananias asked. "Has he told you, Caleb, his plans for salvation?"

Caleb scoffed and left the square. Three or four others followed him.

And then, it was as if a great wave washed over Jonathan. The remaining elders all rose and came close; they touched the sleeves of Jonathan's tunic, mussed his hair, shouted words of encouragement and congratulations. Finally, they hoisted him onto their shoulders and began to sing hymns. Jonathan swayed from side to side and held the celebratory basket high above his head. In this fashion, they all marched back to Eli's house where Eli's wife rubbed her hands on her apron and nervously surveyed the crowd.

"I'm sorry, Sapphira," Jonathan shouted above the din, "it just *happened*. I don't think they mean to stay." And they didn't. They lowered Jonathan back to the ground and exchanged blessings with Eli. Then, babbling merrily, they disappeared into the darkness, heading for their separate homes.

It took hours for Jonathan to fall asleep.

Overruling her husband, Sapphira let Jonathan sleep for most of the next day. By Friday, however, the boy had recovered fully and was eager to see more of the city. Especially since the Passover celebration was now nearing its climax.

Jonathan thanked his cousins profusely, but insisted he wouldn't presume any further on their hospitality. He assured them he knew his way to the Temple. And he knew how to get back to Bethsaida.

"At least let me give you something for your basket," Sapphira said.

Jonathan assured her this was unnecessary, but Sapphira would not take no for an answer. "A gourd of water, Jonathan—you will certainly get thirsty." This was true enough. "And bread; you can't go far without bread."

Though embarrassed, Jonathan was grateful when Sapphira filled his basket.

"And two sestertii," Eli added, shoving the brass coins into Jonathan's palm.

"I couldn't," Jonathan said.

"You must," Eli insisted.

Soon Jonathan was off, again twirling and skipping over the cobblestones. The crowds were even larger and more boisterous than on the day of his arrival. A palpable excitement filled the air, a *tension*. What was its source, Jonathan wondered. Everywhere he saw soldiers, many more than Jonathan had ever seen in one place. Soon he ran into a great wall of them; standing shoulder-to-shoulder at the side of one of Jerusalem's main streets. They seemed to be expecting some sort of procession. Maybe the prefect himself. But no, Jonathan soon discovered. Instead the soldiers were keeping the way clear for a prisoner and his guards. There was just one prisoner, so far as Jonathan could tell. The noise was deafening, dominated by moaning and tears, which was natural enough, Jonathan supposed. The man must have family and friends. And the man was carrying a wooden beam, and struggling with it. It couldn't have been easy. Ah, Jonathan realized! So this is what a crucifixion looked like! Was it common practice to make the prisoner carry his own cross? Jonathan shook his head. He did not understand cruelty. He had never understood it. Even thinking of it, made him feel like someone had punched him in the stomach.

Finally, the unhappy procession passed directly in front of Jonathan, who did his best to peek between the shoulders of impassive Roman guards.

"Master!" Jonathan cried out, recognizing Jesus.

Jesus had fallen to one knee and was breathing hard. It seemed as if all of humanity had gathered in this one city block—voices yelling, crying, encouraging, insulting . . .

"Master!" Jonathan repeated, momentarily slipping through a small gap in the line. He had little hope his single voice could penetrate the confusion. Yet, somehow, Jesus met his stare.

There was a trickle of blood dripping from Jesus's left temple, and on his head lay a crown of woven brushwood. Everywhere his face was stained with sweat. Yet, for all that, in the Master's eyes there was—what could you call it? Jonathan had never seen such a look. Almost as if he were calm. Jonathan could not believe it—enduring all this—still the Master seemed at peace. Not without pain, clearly, but still . . . somehow *hopeful.* Jonathan fumbled, at a loss for words or deeds. Suddenly he reached for his basket and broke off a piece of bread, holding it out. It was a stupid, pointless gesture but. . . .

"What do you think you're doing?" one of the soldiers demanded in barely intelligible Greek, at the same time kneeing Jonathan in the back. Squeezing shut his eyes to absorb the pain, Jonathan stretched out his hand a second time.

"Are you deaf? Get back behind the line!"

Time was brief. Jesus managed the tiniest of smiles. His words would have been lost in the din, so he just moved his lips, forming two words, two distinct words aimed directly at Jonathan.

Two soldiers grabbed Jonathan under the arms and threw him back behind the line, adding a punch in the ribs for good measure. The contents of his basket lay scattered on the street and Jonathan scrambled to recover what he could. On his knees, amid the sea of nervous legs, Jonathan's eyes came to rest on a little girl, tattered and dirty, maybe two years old. What was she doing here? She should be somewhere else, somewhere safe! Where were her parents?

The little girl had the largest brown eyes Jonathan had ever seen, and they pierced through him more deeply than a Roman spear.

Jonathan had once had a young sister. Much like this. Tear-stained, hungry; she did not live long.

It was as if the two of them were enclosed in a perfect little bubble— the world of confusion, hate, and sorrow, temporarily put aside and muted. Not wanting to scare the creature, Jonathan did his best to wipe the dirt and sweat from his forehead. He had a cut on his cheek which he stanched quickly with his sleeve.

Smiling, Jonathan held out his hand. He did his best not to tremble. He opened his fist and offered the bread. He did not know what else to do.

"Don't be afraid, little one," Jonathan whispered. "Take some. Eat."

Born Again

Normally there would be a procession, and great wailing, and a rending of clothes, but today there was only the soft rustling of grey-green olive leaves and the clip-clop of his donkey's hooves scrambling over the stony ground. Nicodemus leaned close to his donkey's right ear. "The cave is just around the corner, my friend; then you may rest."

He was not without sympathy for the animal. The donkey was old, like himself, and carrying a considerable load. Nicodemus's rough hands patted the donkey's rough head. "There, there, you are a faithful companion; let no one deny it."

His wife might. "Who talks to a donkey?" she would ask. "And he is *not* your friend." Nicodemus would stare at the ground, nodding in reluctant agreement. "Has he not several times kicked you in the thigh?" It was the knee, but Nicodemus did not correct her. "For Heaven's sake, Nicodemus, he is just an animal, so *treat* him like an animal."

Nicodemus began to unload the bags of spices—seventy-five pounds altogether, he guessed. Plus clean water. More than enough—but then, in such a case, it was much better to have too much than too little.

A noise from the cave's entrance startled Nicodemus. (Of course, it was no mere cave. If the rumor was true, it was now the burial place of the Master.) "Who's there?" Nicodemus asked. He stepped backwards and stumbled over a rock. He had to grab his donkey's neck to keep his balance; from there he pulled himself around to its opposite side, using the animal as a shield. "Sorry, old friend," he whispered.

Nicodemus squinted and shaded his eyes from the sun to get a better view. He could hear his own rapid breathing and the much calmer breathing of his donkey. If he had to flee on foot, it would be hopeless. His legs had turned to mush.

Finally, two eyes peered out from the cave's darkness, followed by a hesitant torso and upraised hand. "Peace to you, brother," the ghostly figure said. It was no Roman, praise the Lord, nor a colleague from the Sanhedrin. Nicodemus put a hand to his heart, telling it to slow down—all was well.

Finally, the stranger, a grey-beard like himself, stepped into the full sunlight. "I am Joseph. From Arimathea. You're just in time."

Nicodemus stepped out from behind his donkey. "Then it is true!" He had heard the rumor, yet could scarcely believe it: how this man—this simple man—not even a rabbi, but clearly a follower of the Master—had met with the prefect himself. How does one do such a thing? And then asked for the body of Jesus. And finally brought it for burial in his own family tomb!

"Brother," Nicodemus called out, "it is good that we meet. My name is Nicodemus."

Joseph smiled. "I know who you are."

Nicodemus looked behind him. One must always be wary.

Joseph held out both hands. "Shalom, rabbi; your good works walk before you. As you say, it is good that we meet."

There was a clattering of hooves, and again Nicodemus shot a glance behind. His donkey was no fool. He had moved under the shadow of an olive tree and was munching blissfully on a rich stand of grass. Good for him. If his donkey showed no alarm at this stranger, why should he?

"Have you come to help prepare the body?" Joseph asked.

Nicodemus nodded cautiously. It was not too late to change his mind.

How often in his life had Nicodemus found himself in situations like this—where he desperately *wanted* to help, and yet hesitated.

Joseph smiled. "You've brought spices, I see."

"Nard, aloe, a little myrrh—whatever I could get my hands on quickly."

It took them three trips to move the weighty bags into the tomb. They left a trail along the ground where they had dragged them, evidence, for anyone who cared to look, of their sympathy for a man officially branded a criminal of Rome.

At first, Nicodemus could see nothing. But slowly the stone recess, and the body that lay in it, solidified out of the gloom. A single lit candle sat at the head, and another at the foot. The detail it illuminated was almost too much to bear.

Before him was no rumor. Here lay Jesus of Nazareth, quite still, forever still, nail wounds clotted, but clearly visible on hands and feet. As any man his age, Nicodemus had seen many dead bodies, and had presided over many a shiva. But always, when all was said and done, the prayers and hymns completed, Nicodemus felt an inconsolable dread. Death, the final unavoidable indignity. Words of consolation were always on his lips—his training ensured this— but when he looked into his own heart, he found only emptiness there.

As for the reassurance of a happy afterlife—he had his doubts.

The Master's arms were folded across his chest, in a gesture that suggested he was ready to receive a blessing—except none would be forthcoming. No blessing received, and none given. These legs, which had strode so confidently along Jordan's banks, would stride no more. These nostrils would no more know the scent of wild thyme on the Galilean hills. And these lips, from which words flowed like fire and honey, would speak no more. *Blessed are the poor in spirit*[91] . . . *blessed are those who mourn*[92] . . . *blessed are those who hunger and thirst for righteousness.*[93] Words as ethereal as windblown chaff, Nicodemus feared.

Joseph shrugged sadly. "I have started the washing, but as you can see. . . . " Joseph winced. "It is such a blessing you came with your spices."

Nicodemus nodded, understanding his duty. While Joseph worked at another niche, unwrapping linen, he began infusing several vessels of water with his spices. They had two hours left, no more.

It was not the first time Nicodemus had washed a dead body, though he had always thought it a duty better fitted to women, whose gentle touch no man could match. Still, if not he and Joseph, who else would do it? Time was short. Nicodemus's damp aromatic sponge moved up and down the Master's arms, his legs, his sides and gently across his forehead.

"Shall I do the hair?" Nicodemus asked.

"Please," Joseph answered.

With bronze scissors Nicodemus carefully trimmed Jesus's hair. It was quite possible it had never looked as neat. For good measure, he put another layer of myrrh across Jesus's forehead.

Finally, Joseph returned with the linen, ready to start wrapping the Master's limbs.

Joseph kept his eyes on the lifeless body, concentrating on the job at hand—winding, lifting. Precise and gentle, he started with the feet. "You knew the Master?"

"I had occasion to speak with him." The memory haunted Nicodemus. "Twice."

"Then blessed are you," Joseph answered.

The work developed a rhythm of its own—Joseph winding the linen over and Nicodemus pulling it under and handing it back to Joseph.

"What did you talk about?" Joseph asked.

To this day, it shamed Nicodemus deeply—how, like a thief, he had sneaked through the night, dashing from one street corner to another, hiding in the shadows. Finally, he met up with his "contact" who told him the Nazarene awaited him in an upper room.

"Did the Master speak to you in parables?"

Nicodemus shook his head. "I might have preferred a parable, but no."

"What did he say exactly?"

Nicodemus paused; he had never before shared this conversation. "He told me . . ." Nicodemus grunted softly and shook his head—even now the words challenged everything he knew. "He told me I must be born 'from above'. "

Joseph looked up from his work. "From above?"

"Born again, I suppose."

Joseph looked around the tomb as if in some dark corner an explanation might lay hidden. "Is a man to re-enter his mother's womb?"

How stupid Nicodemus had felt at that moment, especially when Jesus went on to ask: "*Are you a teacher of Israel, and yet you do not understand these things?*"[94]

Nicodemus had felt stupid ever since. The notion hung over him like a dark cloud wherever he went. There were so many things he did not understand—and he, a Pharisee, meant to instruct others. He put a hand over Joseph's arm. "I think the Master meant we must be born not just of the flesh, but also of the spirit."

Joseph nodded slowly and sagely, as befitted his long grey beard, but it was quite possible he didn't know what these words meant either. He returned to his work.

They had almost reached the Master's knees when, once again, Nicodemus stopped Joseph, putting a hand on his arm. He tilted his head in the direction of the tomb's entrance where the lowering sun sent a shaft of golden light inside.

"We have to stop," Nicodemus said. "We can return after the Sabbath."

Quickly they gathered their things and moved to the cave's entrance.

"Help me roll this stone," Joseph said.

The stone was heavy and not as circular as they would have wished. It was hard work for two old men to move it, but they managed.

Nicodemus stared at the olive trees which were now deep in silhouette. Pink-tipped clouds flecked the saffron sky. It would be touch-and-go whether they would make it home before sunset.

So, Nicodemus thought, pausing for a moment to wipe his brow and catch his breath, *this was how it would end: light, hope and life itself, fading into everlasting darkness. This was Man's lot. This was the lot even of Jesus of Nazareth, Son of Man.*

Nicodemus's donkey pawed at the ground and brayed loudly at his approach—but not in the usual way—not in complaint. It was more like a friendly greeting, a reassurance even. With the donkey's lips pulled back and his great white teeth showing, it could well be mistaken for—not that he would ever tell his wife—a smile.

"Back home, my friend!" Nicodemus shouted to his donkey, patting him on the head as he spoke. The golden sun hung like a polished chalice in the west. Nicodemus paused in wonder; he cocked his head and frowned; a seemingly pointless question seized his thoughts and would not let go. Wake a man from a long sleep, he asked himself, and could he tell the difference between a sunset and a sun*rise*?

Empty

It was mid-morning and Jesus was dead. Behind a bolted door sat a scattering of dejected apostles. Peter had told them to close all the shutters, and yelled at them when a stray beam of light found its way through a shutter not closed tightly enough.

Thaddeus spoke in a quivering voice: "They're sure to find us, aren't they?"

Peter glared at him. "I told you to be quiet."

"And then they'll crucify us."

"I said, *be quiet.*"

"I am as ready to die as the rest of you, but I don't want to be crucified!"

Peter stood and pounded his fist on the table. "How am I to think, man, if you keep babbling away!"

Thaddeus jumped back, pressing up against the safety of John's shoulder.

Quickly they all dropped back into a gloomy silence. Peter sat back down and let his damp head fall to the table. He wrapped his head in his hands.

Crucified, Peter was thinking, could it be a worse fate than being abandoned? Abandoned and ashamed. Utterly desolate. Peter's great dark hands hid his tears, which had gathered in a pool on the table.

It was all one never-ending, bad dream. All his life Peter had been prone to crazy, disturbing dreams, and did all he could to put them off by staying awake. But when it had most mattered, he had failed utterly! How the Master's words stabbed at his heart! "*So, could you not stay awake with me one hour?*[95]

Why could Peter not stay awake? Why, upon the Mount of Olives, did sleep overcome him like a heavy cloak, and remove him from the world of men? Not just Peter—James and John too. All of them! Useless! Three times the Master had to wake them. Peter groaned and rubbed his eyes, forcing himself awake. *"Get up, let us be going,"* Jesus said. *"See, my be-trayer is at hand."*[96]

Surely the one to betray the Master was *Peter himself* who could not keep awake and pray with Jesus! It was a simple request. What any friend would do for another.

Peter sobbed out loud at the memory, then growled loudly to disguise his outburst. "Quiet, I say! I am thinking!"

All his thoughts, like hungry rats, nibbled at his brain. Why did he not see it coming? Why did he not understand what Jesus told them would happen? And why, oh why, did Peter do nothing to prevent it?

Eyes still closed and head pressed against the table, Peter reached down to feel his blood-stained sword. It was still there, another bitter memory—his feeble, last-moment attempt to actually *do* something. Not yet fully awake, he'd swung it wildly. It came down on the side of a servant's head, catching his ear. Peter was ready to die in that moment. Did the Lord not understand this? *They shall have to kill us both*, he wanted to yell out. But then Jesus turned and looked to him. All the universe was reduced to this small circle of men. "Peter, *put your sword back in its place,"*[97] Jesus whispered. And his voice was so calm, so heart-wrenchingly *calm*!

Another sob escaped Peter's lips; he made no attempt to disguise it. His arms began to shake at the nightmarish memory of his time in the court-yard of Caiaphas. How bitterly cold it was. No matter how close Peter stood by the fire, it could not seem to warm him. And what was everyone *doing* there anyway? Did they come to gloat? To celebrate the Master's arrest?

Peter held his cloak up to his face, trying to go unnoticed. *"You also were with Jesus of Nazareth,"*[98] a servant girl said. Peter pulled the cloak higher, answering in a gruff voice: "You're speaking nonsense!" Peter began slowly walking away, but not too fast, not wanting to draw attention to himself. Then another young woman spotted him. "There! That's one of them." She pointed. *"This man was also with Jesus of Nazareth."*[99]

Peter cursed the girl and all those who listened to her: "I tell you, *I do not know the man!"*[100]

Peter quickened his pace. The exit wasn't far. By now, a large crowd was staring at him. One of them shot out a finger: "Who are you trying to fool? *Surely you also are one of them, for your accent betrays you."*[101]

Peter screamed at the top of his lungs: "Are all of you deaf? The man is a stranger to me!" It was at this moment that the rooster crowed.

Lord, Lord, forgive me! Peter collapsed into a grief beyond words, letting his arms splay out across the table and his face crush against the darkened wood.

There was a knock on the bolted door. All the disciples stiffened. Thaddeus rose to his feet, but John grabbed his arm and made him sit.

They heard another knock, urgent, but not heavy, not what one would expect from a Roman soldier or a temple guard.

James stood—recklessly, thought Peter. Even more surprisingly, he pushed away from the table and tiptoed toward the door.

Philip asked for all of them, "James? What are you doing?"

James crossed the room and put his lips close to the door. "Who's there?" he asked.

The voice on the other side answered: "It's Mary!" No soldier or guard, thank Heaven. Cautiously, James opened the door. The disciples had to shield their eyes against the great blast of sunlight that rushed in. The silhouettes of three women stood in the doorway: Mary the mother of Jesus, Joanna, and Mary Magdalene.

"Quickly, quickly, come in!" James said.

The women were smiling; it made no sense.

"We've just come back from the Master's tomb!"

How, Peter asked himself, could this be the source of good news?

Joanna spoke next: "We'd brought spices with us, though we had no idea how we would roll away the stone."

Mary Magdalene's smile was totally inappropriate, inexplicable. "*But,*" she said, "the stone had already been rolled away for us!"

"By whom?" Philip asked.

Jesus's mother plunged ahead. "And inside, the tomb was empty!"

"What do you mean 'empty'?"

"Jesus was not there, Philip!"

Mouth open wide, Thomas seemed ready to demand further explanation. Joanna ignored him. "When we came out of the tomb again, we saw two men, all in dazzling white clothes—"

Peter whispered to himself, "Brighter than any laundry."

"They asked us '*Why do you look for the living among the dead?*' "

"What?" Thomas blurted out.

Mary Magdalene grabbed the hand of Joanna and the Master's mother. "Those are the very words the angel spoke to us, Thomas. '*He is not here, but has risen!*' "[102]

The only sound in the room was that of the women's breathing.

Suddenly Peter shot to his feet. Quickly he wiped the salty stains away from his cheeks. He marched to the door, pausing briefly to take the hand of his Master's mother. Then he unbolted the door and flung it wide open.

Philip winced and again shielded his eyes. "And where do you think *you're* going?"

Peter grunted, almost laughed. He did not look back. "Where do you think?"

Loose Ends

The sandals of the governor of Judea slapped loudly against the tiled floor of his portico. He paused to study the mosaic below him: a frisky dolphin surrounded by three bare-breasted sea nymphs. A young man, his arms filled with booty, sat upon the dolphin's back, and it was clear that this curly-haired, laughing hero was on his way home. And home meant Rome. At least that is how Pilate chose to interpret the scene. Who would *not* want to return to Rome? And with one's arms full of loot? After all, was it not his right as prefect, as the man in charge of this whole cursed province?

Pilate sat heavily in his chair. Its curved arms made it look as if he were sitting in the middle of a giant, cushioned, stringed instrument. It was an exquisite piece made of polished Lebanese cedar, with inlays of ebony—essentially a throne—it would not look out of place on the Palatine.

Pilate's wife, attired in her best pleated chiton, and with her hair magnificently coifed, stared out at the sea. Pilate noticed she hadn't bothered to put on her stola. She seldom did in the company of just her husband. The stola made Procula look frumpy, which in fact she was. But Procula needn't be reminded of the fact.

From the balcony one could see the greater portion of Caesarea, its red-tiled roofs, its symmetrically arranged streets, its columns, temples, baths and theaters, all a good approximation of what a Roman town should be. Except it was *not* Rome. Despite Herod's best efforts (and, to some extent, Pilate's too) Caesarea remained a hopeless backwater.

"Staring out at the sea won't shorten our stay, Procula."

Procula did not turn. "We don't belong here, Pontius."

Pilate glared "You *think*?"

The governor raised a hand and, in two beats, a young Syrian boy was at his side with a bowl of dates. Two steps behind him stood a second boy with a goblet and jug of wine.

"You should not have executed him."

Pilate finished chewing his date. "I beg your pardon?"

"The Nazarene."

Pilate glared and leaned forward. "As you'll recall, it had never been my intention to execute the *Nazarene*—as you call him—but my hands were tied. In ways, I doubt I could make you appreciate."

Turning, Procula returned her husband's glare. She seemed determined to make a contest of it.

Pilate obliged. "Why are you even concerned about the matter? It's finished. One more Passover done and gone, and Jerusalem at our backs, thank the gods." The date in Pilate's mouth seemed tasteless. "And don't try that silent treatment with me—I had quite enough of that with the so-called King of the Jews."

"You ignored my dream."

"Your dream!" Pilate spat out his date pit. Boy Number One scrambled to retrieve it. "You expect me to govern according to my *wife's dreams*?" Pilate engaged his sarcastic tone, the rhetorical device most suited to his personality. "*My wife's dream told her I must not harm the Nazarene, so I must listen to her DREAM!*" In one gulp, Pilate drained his cup. Cautiously his cup-bearer, Boy Number Two, began to refill it. "Slop over a single drop," Pilate warned, "and I'll make you lick the spill from the floor."

Procula sat behind her loom, fancying herself some long-suffering Penelope, no doubt. Pilate spoke with knife-cutting clarity: "We have servants for that kind of thing."

Procula didn't answer.

"You think it's easy?"

Very softly Procula said, "Weaving?"

"Governing!"

"As I recall, Pontius, you begged Tiberius for the post."

"Yes, but not *Judea*! Of all places! Great Jupiter, we'd be better off in Britannia or Dacia."

"Where blue-painted savages could cut our throats?"

"Blue or not, they can cut throats equally well in Judea. And have done!"

Procula began to move her hands: back and forth, in and out.

In response, Pilate began tapping his fingers against the arm of his grand chair. "Surely you could find a pastime less distracting."

"You needn't stay."

Pilate rose to his feet. His young cup bearer followed precariously behind. Before his favorite mosaic, the prefect paused, legs astride, ogling, as he always did, the scene of Venus rising from the sea foam—the goddess of beauty in her full naked form.

"The place is entirely ungovernable."

Procula looked up, but said nothing.

"What else was I supposed to do?" Pilate held out his empty cup. "I gave the wretched man every opportunity to recant. '*Are* you the king of the Jews?' I asked. More than once. 'Just tell me plainly, *are you* the *King* of the *Jews*?' It was a simple question." Pilate renewed his pacing, re-living the scene. "But the exasperating Jew wouldn't answer." Pilate drained his cup and flung out his arm for yet another refill. "At first I thought he was deaf, or maybe soft in the head. 'Let me remind you,' I said, speaking nose-to-nose, so there could be no confusion, 'claiming kingship would amount to a capital offense.' "

Sighing, Procula abandoned her weaving. "Sometimes words are insufficient."

Pilate spun on his heel and thrust a finger toward his wife. "About *that* we are agreed. And if that damned Tiberius would grant me a full legion, I could demonstrate that principle clearly." Pilate snapped his fingers at Boy Number One. "Bring me some figs." Instantly a flurry of receding footsteps echoed down the portico.

"You know what that annoying Jew answered finally?"

Procula allowed herself the barest of smiles. "I was listening in the other room."

"Well, you *know* then. He said his kingdom 'wasn't of this world.' Nice, huh? Didn't *deny* he was a king, but not one that could threaten our *glorious* emperor."

Pilate reversed direction, strode by his wife, and quickly filled up the space on his balcony. Stiffly he rested his hands on the polished marble railing, looking out over Homer's wine-dark sea.

It was never an easy thing sailing across the Mediterranean. Even with the Roman fleet on patrol, pirates were always a concern. And how many ships rested on the sea's bottom thanks to sudden storms? Even one of his own, filled with cargo from Egypt and points south, laden with spices of great value—all lost in a single day. Still, even considering the risks, Pilate would jump at the chance to take passage on the first ship sailing west.

The governor paced, weighing the difference between wishes and reality.

"Who do they think they are, these Jews? Why is it so hard for them to understand they are a conquered people?" With the light footsteps of a small dog, Boy Number One approached with a bowlful of figs. Making no eye contact whatsoever, Pilate grabbed a handful. "And it's not like we don't bend over backwards to accommodate them."

Before starting his posting in Judea, Pilate had been briefed by his predecessor's scribe, one of those Greeks who thought he knew everything. "Prefect," the Greek had said to him, "it is important to be especially sensitive to Jewish religious observances." Pilate raised his eyebrows—why was he being reminded of the obvious? Tolerance toward local customs had long been a cornerstone of Roman foreign policy. Within certain limits, of course. "You understand, Prefect," the Greek went on, "it is very important that no graven images be found in their places of worship."

"Graven images?"

"Images of the divine Augustus—statues, engravings, anything of that sort."

"You can't be serious."

The Greek nodded sadly. Pilate remembered having a sudden urge to slap the man's face.

And the fuss they had made—unfathomable—when Pilate, after two days of weary travel from the coast, had entered Jerusalem. Just because his troops carried the imperial eagle on their standards! In no other place in the empire would this have been an issue! And call it what you will—Herod's Palace was *his* residence in Jerusalem. It did not belong to any Jew. Pilate was fully within his rights to set up his gold shields in honor of his emperor wherever he liked!

How could his own private homage be seen as a provocation? Great Jupiter! It's not like the shields were on public display! But then the bloody high priests wrote to Tiberius to complain! Which wasn't the worst of it; two months later he got a letter back from Rome *scolding* him for his insensitivity!

Mumbling incoherently, Pilate shook his head at the bitter memory. Tiberius was no Augustus—that much was clear.

The much abused governor returned his gaze to the sea, toward Cyprus, the land of Venus, and wished the goddess's foam would wash across his face, his whole body; he wished he could wash his hands of the whole bloody mess they called Judea.

"Gods of Olympus," Pilate blurted out, "I offered them Barabbas; what more could they want?"

Procula looked up, perhaps wondering if the question were rhetorical.

Pilate continued, "Deluded the Nazarene may have been, but he was no terrorist. If they were itching for a crucifixion, Barabbas was the obvious choice."

Procula could smile at the most inappropriate times. "I can see that you were in a difficult position."

"I was!"

"As many a governor before you."

"What's *that* supposed to mean?"

Further argument was suspended, on the arrival of a messenger from Jerusalem. He went down on one knee and presented a scroll.

"What's this?" Pilate asked.

"From Jerusalem, Prefect."

Pilate unfurled the document, moving his lips as he read, then laughed darkly as he finished. He looked down at the messenger whose head remained bowed. "Do you know what this says?"

The messenger shook his head.

"You, Procula? Can you guess?"

She couldn't.

"I'll tell you then!" Pilate flung the scroll to the floor where it wobbled briefly, then slid, till it came to rest against a leg of Procula's loom. "It says the body of the bloody Nazarene is missing!"

"What?" Procula exclaimed, too late to stifle her laugh.

"It's no laughing matter! Somehow, they got past our guards, rolled away a heavy boulder, and stole the body!" Pilate threw his hands up in the air. "How could this happen?"

As a boy, Pilate had had his own personal Greek tutor whose job it was to prepare him for life as a Roman administrator. It had been drilled into him repeatedly to distinguish between the message and the messenger. But Pilate had never thought much of this teaching. Turning to the still kneeling messenger, he shouted, "Did you hear my question?"

"I know nothing of the matter, Prefect."

"Well you should!" Pilate pushed him violently, causing him to stumble. In a moment, he regained his balance and knelt again, changing legs this time.

"No one is accountable for anything in this place! *Let Herod Antipas decide. No, no, try the Sanhedrin, or the high priests, or the street vendor around the corner!*" Pilate's face grew increasingly more crimson. "This makes me look like a fool!"

Pilate walked over to the loom and picked up the offending scroll. "But wait—that's not the best part! It says here that rumors have started that the Nazarene has—a Plautus comedy couldn't be more far-fetched—*risen* from the dead!" Pilate snorted and began pacing in small circles. A wreckage of date pits and figs littered the floor. "*Risen from the dead!* Bad enough we have to fight insurrection, now we have to deal with . . ." (The veins on Pilate's neck pulsed visibly as he searched for the word.) "*Myths! Less* than myths. Bedtime stories! Which these Jews are all too ready to believe!"

But Pilate's mood could turn on a knife edge, if need be. Suddenly calm, he turned to the messenger. He brushed dust from the trembling man's shoulders and asked him to rise. "Return to Jerusalem, find the negligent guards, and bring them to me at once. You understand?"

"I understand, Prefect."

"And round up any of the Nazarene's followers besides."

Procula paused in her weaving. Still smiling, Pilate turned and looked at her, savoring the tension he had created and which only he could defuse. "Good man," he said to the messenger. He patted him on the shoulder, but kept his eyes locked on his wife. Just as he had hoped, she regarded him with astonishment.

The messenger saw his moment, saluted sharply, and left.

Casually, the governor walked back to his quasi-throne. "On the other hand, Procula, it's just as I've always said: it's no concern of ours."

Pilate's smile deepened as he sank back in his chair, fingering the exquisite polished wood on the armrests. He doubted anyone in the Senate had a better chair—how could they? Not Tiberius himself. And the aqueduct he had just finished in Jerusalem—it was first class, all built on his own initiative.

Pilate finished his wine and smacked his lips. He looked forward to the arrival of the fleet of Roman cargo ships due into port any day now. He snapped his fingers and instantly a boy-servant stood on either side of him, ready to do his bidding. His wife had returned to her weaving. A late afternoon breeze began to blow in through the balcony. It was one of those rare moments in life when the prefect was unreservedly content and knew himself to be so.

"Really, Procula, the missing body of a *Jew*? In the great scheme of things, what could be less important?"

Endnotes

1. Luke 1:42
2. Matt 1:20
3. Matt 1:21
4. Luke 2:10
5. Luke 2:11
6. Luke 2:12
7. Luke 2:14
8. Luke 2:48
9. Luke 2:49
10. Matt 3:3
11. Matt 3:2
12. Matt 3:11
13. Matt 3:2
14. Matt 3:11
15. Matt 3:14
16. Matt 3:11
17. Matt 3:3
18. Matt 3:11
19. Matt 4:3
20. Matt 4:4
21. Matt 4:6
22. Matt 4:7
23. Matt 7:7
24. Matt 4:10
25. John 2:4
26. John 2:5
27. Mark 2:5
28. Mark 2:8
29. Mark 2:9
30. Mark 2:10
31. Mark 2:11
32. Psalm 146:8
33. Matt 9:12
34. Mark 5:7
35. Mark 5:12
36. John 4:9
37. John 4:10
38. John 4:11
39. John 4:12
40. John 4:14
41. John 4:15
42. John 4:16
43. John 4:17–18
44. John 4:19
45. John 4:21
46. John 4:23
47. John 4:25
48. John 4:26
49. Matt 8:6
50. Matt 8:7
51. Matt 8:9
52. Matt 8:8
53. Matt 8:10
54. John 1:45–46
55. John 1:47
56. John 1:48
57. Matt 4:17
58. Matt 3:2
59. Acts 3:6
60. Matt 6:25
61. Matt 6:26
62. Matt 6:28–29
63. Matt 7:7
64. Isa 35:5
65. Mark 10:47
66. Mark 10:49
67. Mark 10:51
68. Mark 10:52
69. Matt 8:20
70. Matt 8:22
71. Mark 4:38
72. Mark 4:40

73. Mark 4:41

74. John 11:21

75. Mark 6:23

76. Mark 6:25

77. Mark 5:23

78. Mark 5:30

79. Mark 5:34

80. Mark 5:35

81. Mark 5:36

82. Mark 5:39

83. John 8:4

84. John 8:5

85. John 8:7

86. Mark 9:7

87. The identity of Mary in this story is unclear. It could be Mary Magdalene, or an unidentified sinful woman (Luke) or, as in John's version of the story, Mary of Bethany, the sister of Lazarus and Martha.

88. John 12:5

89. John 12:8

90. Luke 19:38

91. Matt 5:3

92. Matt 5:4

93. Matt 5:6

94. John 3:10

95. Matt 26:40

96. Matt 26:46

97. Matt 26:52

98. Matt 26:69

99. Matt 26:71

100. Matt 26:72

101. Matt 26:73

102. Luke 24:5

Acknowledgements

*D*aily Life in the Time of Jesus has been a tremendous resource in the writing of *Loose Ends*. My copy of Henri Daniel-Rops's book is liberally marked with bright yellow highlighter. Thanks to his work, the smells, sounds, and sights of Jesus's Palestine now occupy a large part of my writer's imagination. I am ever grateful.

I also owe a great debt to my wife, Judy, for her thoughtful and thorough editing of these stories. They have improved immeasurably under her care.

I would also like to thank the members of my writing group (Vera, Ross, Ralph and Diana) for encouraging me to proceed with this project, and for their many useful editing suggestions.

Finally, I want to acknowledge two of my first readers, Joan Ralston and Tobias Jenny who, long before I quite realized what I was doing, recognized my stories as part of the midrash tradition.

www.ingramcontent.com/pod-product-compliance
Lightning Source LLC
Chambersburg PA
CBHW050406030726
47503CB00006B/2055